The Forest Ranger's Husband

Leigh Bale

Love Inspired

Recycling programs
for this product may
not exist in your area.

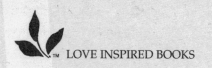 LOVE INSPIRED BOOKS

ISBN-13: 978-0-373-81585-2

THE FOREST RANGER'S HUSBAND

Copyright © 2011 by Lora Lee Bale

www.LoveInspiredBooks.com

Printed in U.S.A.

And Jesus called a little child unto him,
and set him in the midst of them,
And said, Verily I say unto you, Except ye be
converted, and become as little children, ye shall
not enter into the kingdom of heaven.
Whosoever therefore shall humble himself
as this little child, the same is greatest
in the kingdom of heaven.
—*Matthew* 18:2–4

In writing this book, I couldn't help thinking about grace under fire and courage in spite of fear. I know several remarkable people close to my own life who fit this profile exactly. And so this book is dedicated to Daniel, one of my greatest heroes and dearest friends. I love you, son. And to Robin, for having the courage to let her husband serve others overseas even when she needed him more. And also to all wildland fire fighters everywhere. Your guts and skill amaze me.

And thank you to Dan Baird for once again going above and beyond any expectations with his consultation on this book. I've had the time of my life scheming with you!

Chapter One

"Andie, the FCO is here to see you."

Andrea Foster stared at the red light on her telephone console and felt the blood drain from her face. As she held the receiver against her ear and listened to her receptionist's voice, her stomach twisted into knots.

No, Matt couldn't be here so soon. He just couldn't. But he was. Inside the reception area. Waiting to see her. Right now.

She'd known this day would come. Eventually. It was inevitable. But she'd figured Matt would meet someone else and ask her for a divorce, not become a fire control officer working out of the Forest Supervisor's office. She hadn't planned a strategy to deal with him.

The urge to have her receptionist tell Matt she was in a meeting overwhelmed Andie. After all this time, just thinking about him brought so many feelings of anger and hurt to the surface.

It would do no good to send Matt away. He'd just return. They had to work together now. She had no choice. They were having a dry winter, which meant a heavy fire season. Already it was February and unseasonably warm, with very little snowpack in the mountains. As the new FCO, it was Matt's job to ensure her district was prepared. She should get this over with now.

"Andie?"

"Yeah, um, send him in."

Andie dropped the receiver into its cradle. Her arms trembled as she brushed a hand down the front of her drab olive-green shirt and spruce-green pants. The uniform of a forest ranger. The badge pinned to the flap of her left shirt pocket meant a great deal to her. The culmination of a lot of hard work. She felt proud of her promotion over the Enlo Ranger District in Nevada. She'd longed to share the news of her promotion with Matt and even picked up the phone several times to call him, but her fingers refused to dial the numbers. At one time, she'd shared her dreams with him. All her hopes and fears. Now she didn't want him to know she'd met her career goal. It seemed too personal. Too intimate.

She stood and walked past her desk covered with tidy piles of grazing reports and watershed studies. Pausing beside the bookcase, she inhaled deeply, trying to settle her nerves.

Finally. Matt was here.

Now she could tell him what she really thought of him. Her excitement to see him again warred with absolute, utter terror.

And contempt.

He hadn't returned for her. He'd simply taken a new job to build his own career—a job in her hometown. But his return had just hiked her life into a hyper level of complication.

A five-year-old complication named Davie.

A knock sounded on the door. Just before it opened, Andie sat on one corner of her desk, her right leg dangling over the side. She tried to look cool, professional and collected. Tried to appear unaffected by the return of her absentee husband.

Her heart pounded like a jackhammer. She didn't know what to say to Matt. Didn't know how to act. She only knew how she felt inside. Like her heart was being ripped apart again and again.

Clarice, her receptionist, opened the door. Her carefully manicured hand rested on the doorknob as she flipped her long, blond hair over her shoulder. "Here we are."

Matt Cutter limped into Andie's office, his presence like a blast of January wind to the face. In spite of preparing herself, Andie couldn't contain a short gasp. Seeing him after all this time felt like a slug to the gut. She couldn't think. Couldn't breathe.

He gripped a wooden cane in his right hand,

leaning heavily on it. When had he started limping? Was it temporary or permanent?

"Can I get you something to drink? Coffee, water or…something else?" Clarice smiled up at Matt.

He shook his head, his gaze resting on Andie like a ten-ton sledge. In a glance, she took in his forest service uniform, identical to hers. He looked much the same as she remembered him, still slim, broad-shouldered and tall. Except a haunted quality had replaced the cocky, daredevil look in his eyes.

"Thanks, Clarice. I'll take it from here." Andie stood and rested her fingertips on the desktop to help support her wobbly legs. Panic climbed up her throat, but she fought it off. She was a strong, educated, professional woman. She could handle this.

She hoped.

"Hello, Andie." Matt smiled that crooked smile of his, but it didn't reach his eyes.

Eyes the color of cobalt-blue. She remembered their color like her own face. The rich timbre of his voice. His deep laugh. The way his eyes crinkled when he smiled for real.

The taste of his kiss.

Andie felt sick inside. Five years, four months and thirteen days. That's how long it'd been since she'd seen or heard from him. So long that she'd tried to forget they'd ever been married. Tried to forget how much she'd loved him and how furious she was at him for leaving when she needed him more than ever.

She could never forget. Not with a miniature reminder bouncing around her house.

She cleared her voice. "Hello, Matt."

He looked good. Too good. But she needed to keep her distance. Needed to think before she spoke. Even though they were still legally married, this man didn't want her anymore. And she no longer wanted him. She had to remember that. They were married in name only.

"You look beautiful as ever."

Now why did he say that? His words sent shivers racing down her spine, and she realized he'd been perusing her as intently as she had him.

She decided to ignore his compliment. The last thing she needed from him were words that made her love him more. Right now, she'd rather hear an apology.

She gestured toward the cane. "Are you injured?"

"Nothing serious." He sat in a hard-backed chair in front of her desk.

"What happened to your leg?" she asked.

"Just a small battle wound. It'll be fine."

He downplayed his limp, but his strong, stubborn chin hardened slightly. Something about his demeanor told her it was more serious than he let on.

To save her life, she couldn't keep her gaze from roaming over his lean body. He seemed thinner.

Even through the long sleeves of his shirt, she could detect the outline of his strong biceps and shoulders so wide she could have measured them with a broom handle. No doubt he was in the superb physical condition of a soldier. A fire warrior.

A hotshot.

"You still running three miles every day and ten on the weekend?" She used to run with him, though not quite as far.

"Nope. Not until the leg heals. Right now, I'm just walking on a treadmill." He gestured to the cane.

He still wore his jet-black hair shaved on the sides for easy maintenance. High and tight, he called it. But it seemed a bit longer now and shaggy, as if he were letting it grow out. His face looked more mature, the creases in his forehead a bit deeper. It didn't matter. With high, chiseled cheekbones and a curved chin, he was still the most handsome man she'd ever seen.

With the power to crush her heart, if she let him.

Her leather chair creaked as she sat down and leaned back. "What can I do for you, hotshot?"

She meant the name as a derogatory word, not a compliment. When they'd first married, she'd called him hotshot. It'd been a term of endearment then, before he dumped her and actually became one. His raised brows told her he'd caught her sentiment. In his eyes, she detected a glint of arrogance mingled with sadness.

"I'm not a hotshot anymore. Just a fire control officer," he said.

As he stretched one long leg out before him, she couldn't bring herself to smile. Not for all the gold in Fort Knox. All the pain and heartache of the past five years crushed down on her all at once. She brushed a hand across her face, wishing she could hide. Wishing this moment had never come. But it had, and she didn't want to deal with it.

He leaned his cane against the desk, then arched his back as if to ease an ache there. "I don't know if you're aware I was recently promoted to FCO and transferred here to Enlo. We'll be working together."

FCO. The new fire control officer working out of the Forest Supervisor's office.

She kept her face void of expression. "Yes, I heard about that."

An hour earlier, in fact. From an email sent out to all the rangers serving on the Minden National Forest. She still hadn't absorbed the ramifications.

One of his eyebrows arched. "I've been in town a week and thought we should talk."

"About what?"

He tilted his head, his gaze holding hers. "Just talk. There's a lot I need to say, and I want to clear the air between us."

She snorted. "I doubt the air can be cleared with a little chat."

He took a deep breath, his face hardening. "I wanted to congratulate you on your recent promotion. I know being a forest ranger was what you always wanted."

"Yes." Okay, not too gracious, but the best she could muster at the moment. At one time, she had also wanted him and a family, but that hadn't turned out too well.

She didn't like discussing her career with him. Not after all the planning they'd done together during college and the first three years of their marriage. She didn't know this man anymore. He was a complete stranger.

She took a deep breath and let it go. "I just got an email today from the forest supervisor saying you were named the new fire control officer. I can't say I'm surprised you're here in my office, although I didn't expect to see you so soon."

He glanced at the nameplate sitting on the corner of her desk. "I don't think Cal knew we were married when he made the selections for our new jobs. Looks like you're going by your maiden name."

Cal Hinkle, the forest supervisor. If he'd known the connection between Matt and Andie, he undoubtedly would never have brought the two of them in to work together on the same forest. But Andie had started going by her maiden name a year after Matt left, and she rarely talked about her missing husband.

Matt paused, his eyes drilling into hers. "We *are* still married, aren't we?"

She tensed, wishing she believed in divorce. But she didn't. She tried to tell herself that was the only reason she'd never filed, but deep inside her broken heart, she'd always wished he'd return. Now she couldn't help regretting that longing. It'd bring her nothing but more heartache. "As far as I know."

"Good. I never wanted a divorce."

Oh, boy! He'd just opened the corral gate with that remark. "You have a funny way of showing it, Matt."

He took a deep breath. "I know I messed things up between us, but I never wanted to lose you, Andie. I've made a lot of mistakes, but loving you wasn't one of them."

No, no, no! Why did he have to say something like that? It felt like a knife to her heart. Mainly because she didn't believe him. And she wanted to. She really did. But it was too late. "Then why'd you leave?"

"You know why. At the time, nothing was more important than becoming a hotshot crew boss. When I got the job on the Red Mesa IHC, I couldn't turn it down. After we had that horrible fight, and you told me to leave, I figured taking the job was the best thing."

Yeah, which put her in her place. His words meant nothing to her now. When he'd left, his actions had spoken loud and clear. He'd chosen his career over their marriage. Over her.

One of her biggest regrets in life had been when he'd stood on their doorstep with his duffel bag slung over his shoulder. Instead of slamming the door in his face, she should have begged him to stay, or gone with him.

But she hadn't.

She rested an elbow against the armrest of her chair, trying not to show her hurt. Trying to still the trembling of her chin. "You could have discussed it more with me before leaving. Imagine my surprise when I arrived home that night and found a note from my husband telling me he'd taken a job out of state and would talk to me later. That was over five years ago."

Her voice rose to a shrill pitch. No matter how hard she tried to control her emotions, all the anger broiled around within her, the wound still raw. As if it had just happened yesterday. She didn't know if she'd ever recover from such a harsh slap to her face. If he'd left her for another woman, she might have understood. She could have moved on. But his career had become his mistress, and his life didn't include room for his wife.

"I wish I could go back in time and change things," he said.

"Yeah, I'm sure. I think we both said things that

day that we shouldn't have, but it doesn't change things now."

"I'm sorry, Andie. For everything. I really am."

Her breath escaped her in a *whoosh*. Finally the apology she'd longed to hear for years. But it was too late. It'd been too long. He'd chosen his work over their marriage. She couldn't forget that. Could never trust him again. The love she'd kept buried deep within had been trampled to pieces, and she refused to be his doormat ever again.

She had to think about Davie now.

The burn of tears caused her to look away, and she shrugged. "We married too young. You weren't ready for the commitment. Now it doesn't matter. You have your job to do and I have mine. We'll keep our relationship completely professional. Nothing more."

She didn't love him anymore. She didn't. He'd killed her feelings for him, but she didn't know how she was ever going to work with him every day and pull it off.

He frowned, his eyes filled with an emotion she couldn't discern. Disappointment maybe? Surely not. He'd left her, after all. He'd gotten what he wanted.

One question pounded her brain. Why had he left the job he loved? Why had he taken this job as an FCO? Sitting in an office every day. Providing fire support to the various district rangers serving on the Minden National Forest instead of working out on the front lines where the action was. It didn't sound like him. At the age of thirty-two, he was still young and strong enough to run with the best hotshots the nation had to offer. Did it have something to do with his limp?

Hmm. She sensed something wrong here. Something she didn't understand. Maybe she should make a call to find out.

No! She didn't care. His life was his business now. She wasn't part of it anymore.

He leaned forward, his eyes filled with some emotion she didn't understand. "I was hoping maybe you and I could have dinner tonight. I'd like to talk about our—"

The door burst open without warning. "Mommy! Look what Auntie Sue got me."

Davie ran inside wearing a red cape tied over his winter coat and carrying a Rocketman toy figurine. With the accuracy of a stealth bomber, he headed straight for Andie. His rubber boots tracked muddy water across the floor.

"Davie! Remember we talked about knocking before you barge through a closed door?" Even Andie's stern voice didn't stop the boy. He raced around her desk and flung his arms around her. She couldn't resist hugging him back.

Great timing. This situation just kept getting worse. The last person Andie wanted in her office right now was her five-year-old son.

"Davie, I said wait." Susan panted as she chased

after her nephew, carrying her seven-month-old baby in her arms. She came up short when she saw Matt sitting in the office, and her mouth sagged open in shock.

"Sorry! I forgot the rule," Davie said. He held the toy before Andie's eyes, begging for her attention.

Under normal circumstances, Andie would have smiled at his endearing face. She glanced at Matt, whose razor-sharp gaze narrowed as he stared at the boy. She could almost see his mental calculations clicking away. Davie had called her mommy. Matt must be wondering what was going on.

Andie almost groaned. "Susan, you remember Matt."

Sue recovered fast and glowered at Matt, shifting the baby on her hip. "I vaguely remember you married a no-good scoundrel by that name. He abandoned you after three years of marriage and we never heard from him again. The resemblance is amazing."

Andie scowled at her sister and inclined her head toward Davie. Even if Matt had been gone for years, she didn't want her son hurt by disparaging remarks.

A composed smile creased Matt's cheeks. He looked completely calm and even-tempered. Not at all what Andie expected. "Hello, Sue. I see you're just as charming as ever."

"And you've been absent for a very long time.

What are you doing here?" Sue peered at him over the baby's head, her eyes filled with disapproval.

He nodded at the baby who chewed a chubby fist and gurgled. "You're married with a baby of your own now?"

"Yeah, we all kept living after you left, Matt. Life went on without you. Imagine that." Her hazel eyes flashed with anger.

"Sue, watch it," Andie warned with another nod toward Davie.

"Mommy, look at my toy." Davie waved the action figure in front of her face, seemingly oblivious to the adult conversation around him.

Matt's gaze swung back to Davie, and his eyes narrowed.

"Wow! That's great, sweetheart. But I thought you were going to the park after Aunt Sue picked you up from kindergarten." She emphasized the word *park* and tossed an irritated scowl at her sister, wishing more than anything that Sue hadn't brought Davie here.

Sue tilted her head, her hostile glare chewing Matt to pieces. "That's what we planned, but Davie insisted I bring him here to show you his new toy first."

"Hi! I'm Davie. Look what I got."

When had Davie moved over to stand beside Matt? The boy thrust his hand forward, the Rocketman figurine clasped in his small fist.

Andie fought the urge to run over, scoop up her son and take him home.

Fear almost overwhelmed her. Fear that Matt would try to take Davie from her. Or that he'd push the little boy away, just like he'd pushed her away. No way would Andie allow Matt to hurt her son.

Matt lowered his head, gazing into the boy's eyes like he was looking at a ten-million-dollar bill. Miraculous.

"That's pretty cool." Matt took the toy into his hand, but his gaze continued to rest on Davie. An undeniable smaller replica of Matt. "I had a GI Joe when I was your age, but I don't think they make them anymore."

Andie bit her bottom lip as Matt reached out and rested his hand on Davie's shoulder. The boy's impish nose screwed up with a frown. "What's a GI Joe?"

"It used to be the best toy a kid could have. A GI Joe was a soldier and could save everyone. I think your mom still has one."

Andie's mind raced. Boxes of Matt's stuff stood stacked along one wall of her garage from her recent move. No doubt the toy could be found inside one of them.

"Mom doesn't have a GI Joe. I'd know about it if she did." Davie spoke with confidence, as if he knew everything about his mom and her life. A typical kid who believed life for everyone began the day they were born.

"I gave it to her years ago, before you were born. She may have gotten rid of it."

No chance. Against her better judgment, Andie had kept every single thing Matt had left behind when he took off for Oregon. In spite of Sue's disapproval, she'd lugged his stuff with her when she'd transferred to Enlo eight weeks earlier. She didn't know why. Maybe it was time to get rid of it, but somehow she felt as if throwing his things out would also throw away the good memories they'd once shared. And her memories were all she had left. That and Davie.

"Yeah, Mom throws a lot of things out. Aunt Sue calls her the Neat Freak. Can I have my Rocketman back now?" Davie asked.

"Sure." Matt handed the toy back before rustling Davie's dark hair.

Hair the same color as Matt's.

Matt's gaze sought and locked with Andie's. She froze, her mind filled with a jumble of words she longed to say, but couldn't make sense of right now.

Sue stepped toward Davie. "Um, maybe I'll take Davie to the park now. I'll see you at home in a couple of hours."

Sue took hold of the boy's hand and tugged him over to the door.

"Bye, Mommy. Love you." The boy puckered his lips and blew Andie a kiss, his small face aglow with a smile. The corners of his eyes crinkled just like Matt's did when he smiled.

Andie's heart melted and she returned the gesture. Even with Matt sitting in her office, she couldn't refuse her sweet little son.

Sue tossed one last glare at Matt and made a screwy expression with her eyes before she took the children outside and closed the door. Silence followed, so loud it almost broke Andie's ear drums.

"So you're a mom." Matt sat there, his hands resting on his thighs, waiting for her reply.

She lifted her head and met his steady gaze. "Yes I am."

Chapter Two

❧

"How old is Davie?"

Matt's question shook Andie to the core. He sat in her office, his gaze burning into hers until she felt as though he could see inside her very soul. As though she'd done something wrong and had to bear the guilt, not the other way around.

"He'll turn six in April." She'd give anything if Davie were just one year younger. But that would mean she'd been unfaithful to her husband during his absence. And she hadn't. Not once in all these long, lonely years.

Matt shifted his left leg. "He's mine, isn't he?"

Finally Andie looked away and swallowed. She'd planned to tell Matt about their son eventually. Preferably when Davie graduated from high school and she could be certain Matt wouldn't try to take him from her. The way she saw it, Matt would either disregard Davie completely, the way he'd ignored her, or he would demand visitation rights.

Worst-case scenario, Matt would fight her for custody. Andie didn't want a battle over their son. Not when Davie could become collateral damage.

"He has my eyes and my middle name." Matt's voice held a sharp edge she couldn't deny. His eyes looked guarded and hopeful.

No, surely she imagined that.

Andie exhaled a sharp breath. "How would you know? You never had the consideration to ask how I was for over five years."

"Is he mine?" His voice raised an octave, betraying his urgency.

"Yes. Davie is your son." She bit out the words, unwilling to lie. She hadn't been as active in her faith as she would have liked, but she knew the Lord wouldn't approve of lies.

"Imagine my surprise." Hurt and anger filled his eyes.

It served him right.

"Why didn't you tell me I have a son? Why didn't you call?" he asked.

And that's when Andie lost it. "The phone lines work both ways, Matt. When did you ever call me? I haven't heard from you in years. Not once."

"I called you twice, Andie. Three weeks after I left. I got your voicemail at home each time. When you didn't return my calls, I figured you didn't want to hear from me again."

"I never got the messages." Was he lying? Who did he think he was? He had no right to judge her.

Not anymore. He'd lost that right when he'd walked out on her.

She faced him, her hands clenched as she tried to control her trembly voice. "The day we had our terrible fight, I went to the doctor, then came home expecting to share the joy of my news with my husband. But he was gone. He was too much of a coward to tell me goodbye in person. Instead, he left me a note. A single scrap of paper."

The blood drained from his face, and he sat very still for several heartbeats. "You're right, Andie. I should have called you again. Many times, until I got hold of you."

His admission made her angrier. She wanted to hurt him the way he'd hurt her. To let him have it for all the pain and doubt he'd put her through.

"But didn't I deserve to know I had a son? Why didn't you at least tell me about Davie?" he asked again.

"Because I didn't want you thinking I was using a baby to get you back." The truth tasted bitter in her mouth. She remembered the joy of feeling life growing inside her and giving birth to their child. Alone. The last thing she wanted was a husband who stayed with her out of obligation. She wanted a marriage of love or nothing at all.

"I wish I'd known. I wish I'd been here," he said.

Something hardened inside of Andie. Something cold and unforgiving. They couldn't go back in time. They couldn't change the past. Even with

Davie, she had no intention of letting Matt back into her life. "Well, you weren't."

"So after I left you decided to start going by your maiden name." Matt's stomach clenched when he realized he had a child. He felt dazed and sick by the news. And yet strangely elated, too.

Davie was almost six years old. Matt couldn't fathom all the years he'd missed with his child. His son. Years when he could have enjoyed being a father and husband. Years of happiness with his family. He'd missed it all because of his foolish pride.

"With you gone, it made things easier." Andie didn't smile, staring at him with disdain and—

Dread.

A deep aching loss filled Matt when he thought of all he'd missed. If she'd only told him he had a son, things might have been different. He might have—

What?

Would he have quit the job he loved and come running home? He couldn't blame Andie for being upset. It was his fault. He wished more than anything that she'd told him about their baby, but he'd been the one to leave. He could have called her at work, written a letter or email, or even come home to see her during the holidays. But he hadn't.

He held up a hand, hoping to reassure her. Wishing the fear and hatred would leave her eyes. "I won't try to take him from you, Andie. But I do want to be a part of his life. I'd like to get to know my son."

Her spine stiffened. "I…I'm not sure how that will work. I'd need to talk to him first. To tell him you've returned."

"You mean you didn't tell him I was dead or something like that?"

"Of course not. Maybe that would have hurt him less, but it wasn't the truth. I knew he'd find out eventually that you were alive."

So his son believed his father had abandoned him. Filled with shame, Matt licked his dry lips. He could only imagine how Davie felt, missing his father. Wondering why his daddy never came home, read him stories, bought him gifts, played ball with him or tucked him in at night.

Matt's respect for Andie grew. She could have taken the easy way out and just told Davie his father was dead. But she hadn't. And Matt couldn't help wondering if Davie hated him. Maybe death would have been a better option. Matt should have been the one to die in that last wildfire, not one of his crewmen. At least death was something they all could understand. But not this aching abandonment.

"Thank you, Andie."

"For what?" She bit out the words, her eyes narrowed with anger.

"For having our child. It couldn't have been easy,

raising him alone. I can see you've done a great job with him. He seems like a wonderful kid."

"He is. The best." Tears filled her eyes and she blinked.

"Is he a healthy child? Is he smart?"

"He's perfect. What other kind of child would we make?"

"With you as his mother, I'm not surprised." He wasn't sure if he saw doubt or gratitude in her gaze.

"Were you ever going to tell me about our son?" He couldn't help sounding a tad combative. He had to accept responsibility for his part in destroying his family, but he also felt angry that Andie had kept his son from him.

"I didn't see a need."

Ah, that hurt. But he supposed he deserved it. If he didn't think she'd tear his head off, he would have stood and taken her into his arms. Now wasn't the time. After surviving the wildfire, he'd reevaluated his priorities. If anything, Davie gave Matt a stronger reason to live and to rehabilitate his injured leg.

"When can I spend some time with him?" Matt clamped an iron will on his patience. He wanted to see Davie right now, to study the boy's facial expressions and learn his mannerisms. Matt felt like he'd just become a father. As though the amazing event had occurred only moments ago.

For him, it had. He couldn't believe it. He was a dad!

"I'll give you a call." The angry lines creasing her mouth eased a bit, but the wall of tension remained.

Instinctively he knew if he pushed too hard, she could make it very difficult for him to ever see Davie. Matt wasn't stupid. One claim that he'd abandoned Andie over five years earlier and had never seen his own child wouldn't go over too well with a family-court judge. He didn't want attorneys and visitation battles. He wanted his family back.

Matt reached inside his shirt pocket and pulled out one of his new business cards. He handed it to her and she took it reluctantly, letting it dangle from her fingers like a dead mouse.

"My home and cell numbers are on the back. Call me anytime, night or day. I'll come running." He indicated the cane. "Or I should say I'll come walking as fast as I can."

She didn't smile at his attempted humor.

Taking up his cane, he stood and took a step, hoping he didn't fall flat on his face. His left thigh muscle quivered as he put weight on it, but he forced it to endure. He'd returned to work too soon after the fire, but he couldn't wait to see Andie. He looked at her now, letting his gaze feast upon her pretty face. Her blond hair seemed a bit longer, flipped back in soft waves he longed to touch. She looked down at his business card and her hair swung forward, hiding her profile. He fought the urge to reach out and brush it back. To cup her face with his hands and look into her blue eyes as he kissed her lips.

Words clogged his throat. So many things he wanted to say. So many apologies. But she wouldn't believe him. Not yet. There was just one thing he needed to get off his chest right now. One thing he must say to her over and over again.

"I never should have left you, Andie. I wish I had stayed."

She gave a harsh, disbelieving laugh. Her eyes looked so cold. Devoid of the warmth and joy he'd seen there when they'd first married. "I find that hard to believe."

"I mean it." He met her gaze without flinching, trying to convey the truth of his words with every fiber of his being.

She dropped his card on top of her desk and stood a bit too abruptly before stepping away from her chair. The anguish on her face reminded him of all the pain he'd caused her. He didn't want to see her cry right now. Not when she still hated him.

He opened the door and smiled over his shoulder at her. "You take care of yourself. We'll be in touch soon."

Andie left the office as soon as Matt pulled out of the parking lot. After her encounter with him, she wanted nothing more than to see Davie and hold her son close. To know he was safe at home where he belonged.

Alone in her car, she refused to cry. She'd shed enough tears over this man. Why had Matt returned? She'd moved on with her life and didn't want to resurrect the past.

As she pulled into the driveway of the white forest service house where she lived, she gripped the steering wheel, trying to settle her nerves. She didn't want Davie to see her upset like this.

Susan came outside to greet her. When this ranger district had opened up, Andie had jumped at the job. Sue and her husband lived in Enlo, and Andie thought being near family might be good for both her and Davie. She'd been right.

Andie's younger sister stood on the front step, resting one hand on the porch railing. The grave expression on Sue's face told Andie of her concern. And yet, Andie didn't know what to say. She didn't understand this situation herself.

Taking a deep breath, Andie unbuckled her seat belt and stepped out of her car. She dodged the snow shovel lying on the front lawn.

Bless Sue. She was now a stay-at-home mom and spent her time tending to Rose and Davie and helping Andie get settled here in Enlo. If not for Sue and her husband, Brett, Andie didn't know how she would have made it through the past years alone.

As Andie reached the covered porch, Sue stepped forward and handed her a warm sweater. Sue curled into a wicker chair and indicated Andie should join her. "The kids are fine. Let's talk before I take Rose home."

Andie glanced at the front door, noticing it stood ajar so they could hear the children. "Thanks, sis."

"You okay?" Sue asked as Andie sat down.

Andie draped the sweater over herself. Freezing cold in spite of the warm day, she tried to feel something besides deep, abiding hatred. "I'm fine."

Sue peered at her. "You don't look fine."

"Well, how *do* I look?" A gentle breeze pulsed around them, and she brushed the hair back from her face. She felt chilled and irritated and longed to get out of her uniform and into some comfortable sweats.

"You look pale and distressed."

Andie shook her head, filled with disbelief. "Why did he have to come back? Why couldn't he have stayed away?"

"I don't know. The guy is bad news. What does he want?"

"Right now? To see his son."

Sue pressed the fingers of her right hand against her mouth. "Maybe you need to get a restraining order against Matt."

Andie blinked, reluctant to let this situation get any uglier than it already was. "No, I can't do that. Matt has never, ever threatened me. He's not that kind of man."

"Well, there's no doubt Davie would love to meet his father. Besides Rocketman and baseball, his father is almost all he ever talks about. What about you?"

"I don't know. I think I'd rather go on like before, forgetting I ever had a husband. But I have to think about Davie and what's best for him."

"And do you think getting to know his father is best?"

Andie turned her head, gazing at the drift of melting snow edging the sidewalk. The snow reminded Andie of a long-ago, happier time in her life when Matt had taken her skiing for the first time. "Matt always had his faults. You know he was egotistic and goal-oriented to the point of obsessive, but he was a good man, too. He worked hard, provided well and was always kind and generous to me. I have no reason to believe he'd hurt Davie on purpose."

"You think he's been faithful to you all these years the way you've been to him?"

The thought of Matt being with another woman tore Andie's heart to shreds. If he'd been unfaithful, that was between him and God. "I have no idea. It's not my business anymore."

"Maybe you should ask him."

Andie's eyes widened, and a feeling of horror overcame her. "I'll do no such thing."

And yet she wanted to know. Had he missed her at all while he'd been gone? Or had he found someone else to share the long, lonely nights with?

Sue released a deep sigh. "What if he spends

time with Davie and then disappears again? That would hurt Davie so much."

Tears filled Andie's eyes. She blinked to hold them back. "Then I'll be here for my son. I'll always be here for him, no matter what."

"Maybe you need to talk to an attorney. Just to be safe."

Andie took a deep breath, letting the fresh air clear her thoughts. "Not yet. Matt hasn't asked for anything unreasonable, and I don't want to create a fight over nothing."

"You're surely not going to let him be alone with Davie. What if he tries to kidnap your son?" Incredulity filled Sue's voice, her face contorted in outrage at the mere possibility.

"Of course not. I have no intention of letting Matt have unsupervised visits. At least not until I know what he intends. He just barely found out he has a child."

Sue's shoulders stiffened. "I know. I greatly regret barging into your office like that. It kind of let the cat out of the bag a bit abruptly."

Andie waved a hand in the air, resigned to the situation. "Don't worry about it. It was just a matter of time before Matt found out about Davie. Enlo isn't that big of a town."

A regretful huff escaped Sue's mouth. "I should have claimed Davie was my son."

Andie gave a harsh chuckle. "You haven't been

married long enough. Besides, I won't lie. I have nothing to be ashamed about."

"Maybe I could take Davie away for a while. I could take the kids and go visit Brett's mother in Ohio." She shuddered, as if the thought repulsed her.

Andie laughed. "Your offer is very generous. I know how much you adore your mother-in-law. But no. Davie's still in school. If Matt hadn't found out on his own, I would have told him myself."

"Why?"

"Because he has a right to know about his son."

"Do you think Matt would try to steal Davie?"

Andie shook her head, wrapping her arms tightly around herself. "Matt has a job in the S.O.'s office. He's not going to damage his career by kidnapping his own son."

"Does he want a divorce?"

Andie didn't know the answers to any of these questions, yet they kept rattling around inside her brain.

"I don't think so. He apologized for leaving me. He said he wished he'd stayed."

Sue snorted. "Can you believe that guy? What a loser. He always did have a lot of nerve."

Which was one reason Andie fell in love with him. Matt had been so much fun, and intelligent, too. A true athlete, full of life and hopes and plans. And he worked hard to meet his goals. Definitely not a loser. He'd encouraged Andie to meet her goals, too. He'd taken on additional work assignments to earn her tuition, prepared dinner and helped with the laundry. Andie had adored him at first sight. They'd both enjoyed the outdoors, skiing together, hiking, camping, you name it. She'd never been much of a girlie-girl. She baited her own hooks and cleaned the fish she caught. But with Matt's overt masculinity, she'd always felt feminine and protected by him. Loved. Until he betrayed her by leaving. Seeing him now limping around with a cane confused her, and she wondered again if his injury was permanent.

"No, Matt's no loser," she said. "He was always hard-working, in school and in his career. He's a high achiever who just got his priorities messed up. But he has some very good qualities, too."

Sue leaned forward, her eyes creased with concern. "Do you think he'll take you to court, to try and take Davie from you?"

"No. I'm not sure what he wants, but I don't think he would hurt Davie like that. And if he tried, I'd fight him tooth and nail. No one's ever taking Davie from me. Of course, Matt's probably still in shock, finding out he has a son."

"Good. When I think about how badly he hurt you, I figure he deserves a nice shock." A vindictive smile curved Sue's lips.

Andie appreciated her sister's loyalty, but in all fairness to Matt, he'd been a good, diligent husband when they'd been together. She couldn't fault him there. He'd just forgotten what was really important. When she thought of the angst she'd seen in his eyes when he found out about Davie, she couldn't help feeling sorry for him under the circumstances. He'd missed almost six years of his son's life, after all. But Matt had made a conscious decision to remove himself from her life…and any children she might have.

"What are you gonna do?" Sue asked.

"Wait and see."

"Wait and see what?"

"What Matt does."

Sue dangled one stockinged foot over the whicker footrest. "I don't understand. You cried buckets of tears after he left, Andie. I won't stand by and let him hurt you again."

Andie waved Matt's business card with his phone numbers in the air. She'd scooped it up the moment he'd left her office. She didn't smile as she spoke. "Don't worry, I'm over him. Matt didn't contact me for over five years. He said he'd be in touch. Let's wait and see how badly he wants to see his son."

"I take it you're not planning to call him."

"Absolutely not. If he wants to see Davie, he'll have to call me. I'm not going to pursue it."

If Matt wasn't serious about getting to know his son, Andie didn't want Davie to get hurt. Above all else, she would protect her child. Even if it meant he never saw Matt again.

A satisfied smile curved Sue's lips. "Good girl."

Chapter Three

"How's the leg?" Cal Hinkle smiled at Matt as he limped down the hall leading to the reception area of the Forest Supervisor's office.

Normally Matt worked late, preparing for the summer fire season. He paused as the receptionist locked the front door, the clock on the wall reading 5:17. Matt couldn't wait to get home and put an ice pack on his thigh.

"Great," Matt said. He leaned his shoulder against the wall, trying not to grit his teeth. Using the cane for balance, he refused to give in to the pain. He didn't want his boss to know how bad his leg hurt.

Cal showed a concerned smile, talking low. "And you're keeping up with your physical therapy?"

"Yeah, my new physical therapist is great. I've started walking on a treadmill and doing my exercises regularly."

"And what about the post-traumatic stress?"

"I'm dealing with that, too." In his own way. It didn't sit well with Matt to meet with shrinks to discuss his survivor's guilt. So far, he hadn't told a single soul what happened the day he'd lost one of his crewmen and almost died himself. The horror of the wildfire plagued him, and he couldn't put his thoughts into words. He couldn't relive it a second time.

"Good. If you need to talk, my door is always open, Matt. It'll take time, but I know you can heal both physically and mentally."

"I appreciate that." In the daytime, Matt had no problem coping. At night, his dreams haunted him. Jim should still be here, not him. Sometimes Matt woke up screaming, his body covered in sweat. He wondered if he'd ever feel normal again.

Cal paused before returning to his office. "Fire season will start early this year. I've scheduled a meeting in two weeks with all the rangers on our forest. Will that give you enough time to present your fire plan to them?"

Matt nodded, knowing Andie would be there. "I've already been working on one I think you'll like. It should streamline communication between all of us, the BLM and local fire authorities, and offer better use of our resources. I've also been looking at the contracts each ranger will need in place for equipment and heavy machinery for the fire crews. Next week I'll start visiting each ranger to solidify the contracts and find out if they have any special needs."

"Good. I knew you were the right man for this job. Have a nice evening." Cal clapped his hand on Matt's shoulder.

Matt smiled, pleased to be doing something right. Funny how he always seemed to excel in his job performance, while his family relationships were a different matter.

Placing the cane in front of him, Matt headed outside to his truck. Clouds the color of gray slate filled the sky, and it had been raining. The drive home took less than ten minutes. You couldn't get this kind of commute living in a big city.

Inside his dingy studio apartment, he opened the freezer and took out an ice pack. The dismal surroundings needed lamps and pictures on the walls, but Matt didn't care. He only used his apartment to shower, sleep and perform his leg exercises. He slouched on the Hide-A-Bed sofa and laid the cool pack on his leg. He'd never get used to the chronic pain, although he could endure it. The emptiness in his heart was another issue.

Five days and still no word from Andie. He'd tried to give her some space. To give her time to talk to Davie and make visitation arrangements. Now Matt felt like a caged tiger, eager to see her and Davie again. Filled with fears and doubts. He wanted to take things slow, to give Andie time to adjust to him being back in her life, but he couldn't help wondering if this was how she'd felt after he'd left and never called her. Now he wondered how he'd lived all that time without hearing her voice every day. He'd put her through so much. How could he have been so unfeeling to her needs? He hadn't deserved her. But he'd changed so much since then. If only he could show her that he was a better man now. A man who loved her more than he loved life.

He picked up the remote and flipped on the TV, listening absentmindedly to the news. So far they'd had an extra-dry winter with a weak snowpack in the mountains. In the summer, they'd have a heavy fire season as a result. Already he'd started planning the fire school they were scheduled to host in early May to train summer wildfire fighters. He had no doubt they'd need many before summer ended.

After thirty minutes, Matt tossed the ice pack aside. He changed out of his forest service uniform into some sweats and climbed on the treadmill, hoping the exercise might ease the pain in his leg. It didn't. Even with the special ointment the doctor had given him, the tight skin grafts on his left thigh throbbed unbearably.

"Come on, Cutter," he spoke aloud to himself. "Just one more mile. You can do this. You don't need to stop."

As he forced himself to walk, he gripped the handrails. He briefly considered taking a pain pill, but tossed that idea aside. He didn't need an addiction to deal with right now on top of everything else.

When he finished walking, Matt guzzled a glass of water. His body shook and he lay down on an exercise mat, going through the stretching exercises his physical therapist had taught him.

"One, two, three…" He counted off the repetitions, pushing himself to do an extra set of each exercise. The pain eased, but persisted. The hope of walking without a cane kept him from giving in.

When he finished, he sat on the couch and gave a mental shout of victory. It'd been agony, but he'd pushed himself through the pain. He was not going to be a cripple the rest of his life.

Before he could stop himself, he reached for the phone and dialed Andie's number. He'd memorized it, even though he'd never called her yet. It was time they talked.

"Hello," a man's voice answered.

Matt tensed, his mind running rampant with confusion. It never occurred to him that Andie might have someone else in her life. Just because they were still married didn't mean she couldn't have met and fallen in love with someone else. The thought made him feel strangely territorial. Though he had no right, he didn't like the idea of another man usurping his place with his wife and son.

"Is Andie there?" He didn't know who this man was, but he was prepared to fight for his wife.

Oh, please. Please don't let her have someone else in her life. Not now.

"Sorry, but she's in the shower."

Cold dread gripped Matt's heart. Maybe he'd lost her for good. She deserved to be happy. No matter what, Matt intended to be there for her and Davie, in any way they needed him. But what if Andie wouldn't forgive him? What if he could never make up for what he'd done?

"Is Davie there?"

A pause. "Yeah, one moment."

Matt didn't expect to speak to the boy. He just wanted to know if his son was there, in the same room with another man trying to take his place.

But he didn't really have a place in Andie's life anymore. He didn't have a right to resent another man for loving her the way she deserved to be loved.

The stranger didn't give Matt a chance to say anything else. An awkward moment ensued while the man called for Davie. Butterflies swarmed in Matt's stomach as he waited for the sound of his son's voice.

"Hello."

Such a grown-up voice. Matt loved this boy already.

"Hi, Davie."

"Who's this?"

Matt didn't expect the heavy breathing from the boy. He'd never been around kids much and wasn't used to their ways.

"My name's Matt. You and I met in your mom's office about a week ago."

"Yeah, you liked my new Rocketman."

Matt felt the urge to laugh, the first time in months. "Yes I did. I was calling your mom to find out when I might come over and visit you."

"You can come over now."

"I can?"

"Sure. We're not doing nothing special. Mom's got lasagna in the oven."

Homemade lasagna. Andie's specialty. Nothing better in the world. Matt's mouth watered at the thought of sitting down to eat dinner with his wife and son. But he wasn't foolish enough to invite himself without Andie's say-so.

"It sounds like you've already got company," Matt said.

"Nah, Aunt Sue and Uncle Brett are leaving now. You can come over."

Uncle Brett. Susan's husband.

Matt's skin prickled with relief. For a moment there, he'd been shaking with fear.

"You better check with your mom first." Matt knew better than to get permission from a five-year-old.

"Okay." The phone rattled as Davie set the receiver down.

Matt waited several tense moments, listening to the background noise of the TV set. The evening news, if he heard right. Finally Davie returned.

"Mom doesn't mind."

"Really? You're sure she said it's okay?" Matt couldn't contain his surprise.

"Yeah, I asked her. Do you know where I live?"

"I do." Matt had found that out even before he'd secured his own apartment. He'd driven down Andie's street a couple of times, usually in the middle of the night when he couldn't sleep. He longed to confide in her about the fire. To get the guilt off his chest. But he figured she'd just laugh at him. After the way he'd hurt her, she couldn't possibly care about the demons haunting him.

Most nights, he noticed a light on in the front bedroom of her house. Matt wasn't sure whose room it was. When they'd first married, Andie had suffered from insomnia and usually sat up reading when she couldn't sleep. But Davie was a wild card. Maybe the boy was scared of the dark and needed a light on while he slept. Matt longed to get to know his little son. Was the boy shy or brave? Was he athletic or a bookworm? It didn't matter one way or the other. Davie was his, and Matt loved the child unconditionally for no other reason.

"See ya."

The boy hung up before Matt could say good-bye. He felt a buzz of excitement. He'd been invited to dinner at Andie's house. Thank goodness she wasn't going to fight his visitations of Davie. He'd take it slow and easy, trying to soften Andie's heart. The last thing he wanted was to upset his wife and cause a scene in front of their son.

Matt cleaned up and dressed in faded jeans, a blue polo shirt and tennis shoes. He used to wear cutoffs or shorts when he worked out, but no more. The scars on his legs weren't pretty.

After brushing his teeth, he combed his hair. It was getting longer than he liked. Time to find a good barber in town.

As an afterthought, he splashed a bit of cologne on his face, gritting until the sting passed. Before leaving his apartment, he reached for two packages he had sitting on the kitchen table. He'd bought and wrapped them two days ago, waiting for the right moment to present them to Andie and Davie. Then he drove to Andie's house on the other side of town, feeling anxious and giddy at the same time.

"You must be crazy," he murmured to himself as he put on the blinker, then turned the corner. Being around Andie was suicide, flooding him with regret. He could hardly believe she hadn't told Davie negative things about him. Matt figured most women would bad-mouth their estranged husband. But not Andie.

He parked out front, his gaze taking in the house, white with green trim. A classic forest ranger's house. Andie paid rent and maintained the home, but she didn't own the house. That's how it worked in the forest service.

The flower beds had been freshly raked of dead leaves. He knew Andie hadn't been in town much longer than him, and he guessed she'd started bringing the yard back to life in preparation for spring planting. He expected nothing less. Andie had a green thumb; her academic training had been in plants and minerals. Which worked well with her ranger district, filled with mining and grazing permittees. She knew her job well, and he couldn't help feeling proud of her accomplishment in becoming a forest ranger. A rare breed of only four hundred nationwide.

As he carried the packages up the front steps, Matt caught the tantalizing aroma of dinner cooking. His stomach rumbled and he rang the doorbell.

The sound of running feet came from inside, and then the door jerked open. Davie stood there wearing his Rocketman cape, pajamas and floppy-eared dog slippers. Matt couldn't help wondering if the boy ever took off the cape.

"Hi!" Davie pushed open the screen door, but Matt didn't step inside.

"Is your mom here?"

"Who is it, Davie?" Andie's voice came from the kitchen.

"It's Matt," the boy yelled back.

Andie appeared in the doorway, wiping her hands on a dish towel. She looked casual in faded blue jeans and a T-shirt, her slender feet bare. That's what he liked most about this woman. No fuss or muss, in spite of her penchant for neatness. Memories of their life together flashed through Matt's mind and left him filled with such yearning that he longed to go back in time and undo his decision to walk away. Andie in their kitchen fixing dinner. Andie out in the garden, weeding her tomato plants. Andie with her hair curled and smelling divine as he took her out for a night on the town.

When she saw Matt, her eyes widened. "What are you doing here?"

"I—I—" Matt stammered in confusion.

"I invited him. You said I could." The screen door creaked as Davie pushed it wide.

"I did?" Andie stared at her son, and her knuckles whitened around the dish towel.

"Yeah, I asked if I could invite a friend over for dinner and you said yes." Two deep furrows creased Davie's brow. He looked at his mother like she'd gone daft.

Oh, no. Obviously there'd been a misunderstanding. Matt had known the invitation to dinner was too good to be true.

He shifted the gifts in his left arm, leaning his weight on the cane with his right hand. "Looks like we've both been duped by a five-year-old. I didn't mean to intrude. I can come back another time."

Anger smoldered in her eyes, her gaze darting

between the packages and his face. His pulse hitched into triple time. The last thing he wanted was to upset Andie. He took a step back, planning to bid her farewell and return later when she didn't feel ambushed. Instead, he stumbled and almost fell down the steps. A wrenching cry broke from his lips as he dropped the gifts into the flower bed. His cane clattered to the porch and he staggered against the railing, panting hard.

"Matt!" Andie reached for him.

He bent his head so she wouldn't see the agony in his eyes. The excruciating pain and humiliation.

"Are you okay?"

She hovered beside him, her hands clutching his arm. The warmth of her fingers sent electric shock-waves over his body. He liked the worried tone of her voice, but didn't want her pity. It'd been a long time since someone had worried about him, but he wouldn't use tricks to win her back. He hadn't planned to be so clumsy or for his leg to hurt like lightning bolts hurtling through his thigh. He wanted to be strong. To be everything for his family.

"I'm f-fine. Just let—let me catch my breath." He clenched his jaw, fighting off waves of pain.

She pulled a wicker chair over for him to sit down on the porch. He fell back into the chair, breathing hard as he massaged his thigh muscle with his hand. How he hated showing her this weakness. Hated for her to ever know how he'd gotten to this point.

"Davie, get a cup of water," she said.

While the boy raced inside, she knelt beside Matt, her hands clasping the armrest. "Do you need me to call 9-1-1? What can I do?"

He looked at her anguished face and gritted a smile. "You've done it already. Just give me a moment."

Davie returned, looking serious as he sloshed water over the brim of a red sippy cup minus the lid. Matt chuckled as he accepted the boy's offering.

"Thanks, Davie." Matt drained the small cup in two long swallows. The pain eased by small degrees and his breathing calmed. In spite of the chilly air, sweat dripped from his forehead and he brushed it aside. Andie must have noticed because she stood, her expression severe.

"Do you feel well enough to come inside? I have a recliner where you can elevate your leg."

Davie retrieved Matt's cane and handed it to him.

"Sure. I'm fine." He smiled at the boy, doing his best to reassure them both.

Andie took Matt's arm and helped him inside while Davie held the door wide.

At the threshold, Matt hesitated. "I don't want to play on your sympathies, Andie. I won't come in unless you really want me here. My injury has nothing to do with our marriage."

She bit her bottom lip and looked away, a dead giveaway to her apprehension. He'd learned to read her body language long ago and figured she hadn't changed that much in the years he'd been gone. She didn't want him here.

"Come inside for now. Davie invited you."

Okay, that set some limits. She would honor Davie's invitation. At least for now.

"How did you hurt your leg?" she asked.

"Just an accident. I'll be fine." He wasn't about to tell her the story of the wildfire and the death of his crewman. Not when the guilt still ripped him apart every time he thought about it.

Davie retrieved the packages Matt had dropped in the flower bed and set them on the coffee table. "Is one of these for me?"

Matt smiled. "Yep. The blue one. The pink one is for your mom."

"Why don't you two chat while I get dinner on?" Andie ignored the gifts as she opened the drapes wide. Then she disappeared into the kitchen, leaving him and Davie alone. Easily within earshot. Now and then she peered around the corner, making Matt self-conscious. Obviously she didn't like leaving him alone with the boy. Matt was determined to win her trust.

Davie tore open his gift like a rabid wolf. Matt laughed, pleased by the child's enthusiasm.

"What's this for?" Davie asked as he shredded the delicate paper.

"Your birthday."

"But my birthday isn't for weeks. Mom said I can have a party and invite friends over for cake. You can come if you want to."

Matt would love to be here, but he'd wait for an invitation from Andie first. "This gift is for your last birthday I missed."

"A baseball glove. Thanks!" Davie dug the glove out of the box and put it on his right hand.

"You wear it like this, hotshot." Matt pulled the glove off and put it on the boy's left hand. "Now you can catch with your left hand and throw with your right. You are right-handed, aren't you?"

Matt used his own hands to show the motions in the air.

"Yep. I'm a righty." Davie sat on the sofa and scooted back, smacking his right fist against the palm of his new glove. He watched Matt with intense, wide eyes.

As Matt eased himself into the recliner, he couldn't help wondering if Andie had told Davie who he really was. He eyed the wrapped gift he'd brought for her, wishing she'd open it now. He'd leave it here, and hopefully she'd open it after he left.

"My dad's name is Matt. He's a hotshot," Davie said.

"Is that so?" A lump formed in Matt's throat, and he tried to swallow.

"Yep. He plays baseball like me."

"I love baseball."

The child heaved a satisfied sigh, his big blue eyes unblinking. "You're my daddy."

Matt coughed, his throat dry as sandpaper.

Chapter Four

Matt spoke around the hard lump in his throat. "How do you know I'm your daddy? Did your mother tell you that?"

Davie shook his head. "Mom has a picture of you in her bottom drawer. Sometimes I sneak in and peek at it."

Before Matt could respond, the boy hopped off the couch and padded out of the room. Matt sat there in confusion. Had he said something wrong?

The child returned and handed Matt a picture of him with his arm around Andie, smiling and snuggled together on a large boulder at the Grand Canyon. Their honeymoon. Matt remembered it like yesterday. The best time of his life. They'd been so in love. So happy.

And he'd destroyed it all.

Davie sat on the ottoman. "Mom said you'd come meet me one day. Why'd you leave us?"

Us. Fascinating how Davie assumed he'd always been in his parents' lives.

"I didn't know about you when I left. Your mom had you after I was gone."

"So why didn't you come back?" The boy's eyes filled with awe and dejection at the same time.

Matt's mind scrambled for a legitimate excuse that wouldn't lose him any respect in his son's eyes. "The truth is, I was selfish. I wanted to fight wildfires in Oregon, which meant I had to transfer up there."

"Why didn't you take us with you?"

"Your mom didn't want to move. She wanted to stay in one place and raise a family. I wanted to build my career."

"Can't you stay with us and build your career, too?"

Boy, this kid wasn't making things easy. "It's not quite that simple, son."

His son. A bright boy who was confronting him with the truth while trying hard to understand why his father had left him.

"Mom said you don't want her. You just want to see me."

"That's not true. I want both of you. Very much." Matt spoke around the emotion in his voice, hoping to dispel any misunderstandings right now.

"Really? You mean it?"

"Yes, I mean it."

"Pinkie promise?" The child held out his hand, his pinkie finger hooked slightly.

As Matt looped his pinkie finger around Davie's and they shook, he fought the urge to smile. "Pinkie promise."

Davie tilted his head in confusion. "Mom must not know you still want her. You should tell her."

Or rather, she no longer wanted Matt. He couldn't believe it was too late to win her back. He couldn't give up hope.

"Hey! You want to come to my T-ball game in two weeks? It's the first of the season," Davie said.

Matt flinched, having trouble keeping up with the change in topics. It appeared his son had forgiven him so easily. If only Andie could do the same. "I'd love to."

Davie scooted off the ottoman, his face alight with excitement. "All the other dads come. Brian Phelps says I don't have a dad. Won't he be surprised when you show up? You want to see my uniform?"

Matt's heart wrenched. Thinking about his son growing up without a father almost unmanned him. Matt had so much apologizing to do. So much lost time to make up for. "I'd like that."

Davie ran across the room and disappeared down the hallway. Matt looked up and found Andie standing in the doorway, her eyes filled with annoyance.

"I didn't invite you to dinner, you know." She crossed her arms.

"I know that now. I'm sorry for the misunderstanding. I'm not used to how little boys work."

"Oh, sure you are." She leaned against the wall. "They're just smaller versions of grown men."

Matt sighed with resignation. This wasn't going to be easy. For any of them. In the old days, he would have snapped back at Andie, but he just didn't want to anymore. She must be so hurt and angry. Nothing but remorse and love for her filled his heart. "I suppose you're right. But eventually even grown men grow up."

She stepped away from the wall, her mouth tight with disapproval. "I hope so."

Realizing Matt was watching her, Andie blinked and began picking up toys around the living room. She'd overheard Davie's conversation with Matt and didn't like it one bit. How she wished Davie could get to know his father without becoming emotionally attached. But Davie loving Matt was inevitable. The boy wanted his father. So much. For that reason alone, Andie had let Matt into her house.

Against her better judgment.

"You put him into baseball?" Matt asked.

She shrugged. "He started last year. It's what he chose."

"I guess it's in his blood."

She straightened, a roller skate dangling from her fingers. "Actually, he saw a picture of you playing baseball in college and refused to consider any other sport."

He glanced around the room. "I don't see any pictures of me. Not a single one."

She looked away. "He went snooping and found the photo albums I had put away in the bottom of my cedar chest. He's a bit like you. Intelligent and precocious." She didn't mean it as a compliment. "Once Davie realized you'd played baseball, that was it. He insisted he would, too."

And she didn't have the heart to hide the pictures from Davie. At first, she'd left photos of Matt out, hoping he'd return. After a year, the photographs became a constant reminder of what she'd lost, and she'd finally put them away.

"Smart kid," Matt said.

"Yes, he is."

"I can understand why you didn't want to show him pictures of me."

She turned, her gaze locking with his. All the years of waiting and hoping, fighting off the loneliness and hurt, came boiling up inside her fast and hard. "I didn't want him to hurt as much as I did."

"I'm sorry for hurting you, Andie."

"Yeah, right." She pursed her lips tight.

"I didn't know he existed until a few days ago. And he didn't know me."

She hardened her jaw. "And whose fault is that? You left me, remember?"

"If you'd just called and told me I had a son—"

Davie stood in the doorway, looking between them. He wore his Redhawks uniform, the leather baseball glove firmly on his left hand. His little face crinkled with worry. "Are you guys having a fight?"

Matt flashed a smile and gestured to his son. Davie walked closer and Matt squeezed his arm. "No, we're just having a grown-up discussion, that's all. Hey! This uniform looks great on you. Maybe we can play catch sometime."

Davie's eyes brightened. "How about now?"

"It's dark outside and getting late. You haven't had your dinner yet." Andie turned and folded the burgundy afghan before draping it over the back of the couch.

"How about tomorrow evening after I get off work?" Matt stood and tugged on the brim of Davie's baseball cap.

"Yeah! But aren't you staying for supper?"

Matt shook his head. "Sorry, hotshot. I can't. Maybe another time."

"Ah!" Davie walked him to the door. "Don't be late tomorrow, or it'll be supper time and Mom won't let me go out cause she thinks it's too dark and cold."

"You got it."

Matt looked over the boy's head at Andie. She stood in the middle of the room, feeling harsh and unforgiving. She didn't say anything, wishing Matt would leave. If she told him not to come back, he'd find another way to visit Davie. His work provided plenty of opportunity to schedule meetings where Andie would need to be present.

She refused to be forced to do something she didn't want to do. But getting Matt out of her life again would take a gigantic miracle.

Finally Davie was asleep. After Matt left, the boy had been so wound up, he barely ate any dinner. Dad this and Dad that. Davie had gone on and on about what he planned to do with his father. Andie had never seen her son so animated. Not even on Christmas morning.

Oh, Matt. Please don't hurt us again.

Turning off the hall light, she sat in the recliner and stared at the gift Matt had brought her. A small package wrapped in dainty pink paper with a pretty white bow. Her fingers itched to know what was inside. She remembered the last time he'd bought her a gift—on their third anniversary, three months before he left. An exquisite heart-shaped ruby necklace she hadn't worn since. Sometimes she took it out of the box and held it in her hands, usually at night when she couldn't sleep and was all alone so no one heard her cry.

Standing, she picked up Matt's gift and carried it to the kitchen, where she dropped it into the garbage can. The *thunk* as it hit bottom mirrored her empty heart. It felt good to let it go. To mentally tell Matt no. He couldn't just walk back into her life like this. Her heart no longer had room for him.

Flipping off the living room light, she walked through the dark to her bedroom. She sat on the corner of her bed and folded her hands in her lap, letting the quiet of the house settle her nerves.

She shook her head and stood, retracing her steps to the kitchen. In the shadows, she reached for Matt's gift and pulled it out of the garbage before carrying it back to her room. Taking a deep breath, she closed the bedroom door and flipped on the light.

A quick study of the package showed uneven edges and too much tape. Knowing Matt had wrapped this himself almost made her smile. Almost.

Slowly and carefully, she peeled back the delicate paper to reveal a white box. She found an envelope placed on top of an expensive silver-gilded music box. Taking the music box from the Bubble Wrap, she lifted the lid. The soft tune of "Unchained Melody" filled the room.

Their love song.

She hummed along for a moment, remembering the poignant words so well. She had loved this song in the past. Now the lyrics seemed mournful, filled with longing and loneliness.

Are you still mine?

The words left her feeling empty and depressed.

She closed the lid, her hands shaking. The card rested on the bedspread, beckoning to her.

Her fingers reached for it of their own volition. She lifted the flap and pulled the card free of the envelope. For all his manly ways, Matt had always been a romantic. Cards, flowers and gifts. Before he'd left, he'd never forgotten her birthday or their anniversary.

Before he'd left.

The card was just what she expected. A flowery, mushy sentiment of the heart. But what he'd written touched her like nothing else could.

To my dear wife Andie, for giving me the greatest gift of all. Our son. Love, Matt

She sat there in shock. Not even realizing she was crying until her tears dripped onto the card, smudging the ink.

She sniffed and wiped her eyes, then wrapped up the card and music box and tucked them far away in the highest, darkest corner of her closet. Where Davie wouldn't find them.

Her heart ached. She felt more alone than ever before. What did Matt expect from her? To just welcome him back with open arms? She couldn't do that. Not after what he'd put her through. She believed in God, and forgiveness but she just couldn't let this go. She didn't have that much faith.

She wondered about his leg. Something had happened to him. Something bad. Maybe a car accident or other injury. It must have changed him somehow. He seemed so vulnerable now. So sad.

Clicking off the light, she crawled into bed and stared into the darkness. She hadn't said her evening prayers because she knew if she did, she'd have to soften her anger. And she wasn't ready to offer forgiveness yet, if ever.

In the morning, she'd go about her routine, dropping Davie off at kindergarten before she drove in to work. Then she'd close her office door and make a phone call. It was time she knew the truth.

Chapter Five

"Kendal Albright speaking."

Andie gripped the phone in her office and took a cleansing breath when she heard Kendal's familiar voice. "Hi, Ken. It's Andie Foster, er, Cutter. How are you?"

"Andie! Well I'll be. I haven't talked to you in years. I'm great. How about you?"

"I'm good." She didn't know how to broach the subject on her mind. Kendal had worked with her and Matt years earlier when they'd first started as linespeople working summer wildfires to earn enough money for their college tuition. Ken was Matt's best friend and should know what was going on.

"Congratulations on making squad boss of the Red Mesa Hotshots. I heard about it through the grapevine a year ago," she said.

He paused and took a deep breath. "Actually,

I've just been promoted again. With Matt leaving, I'm now the crew boss."

"That's great." She tried to put some enthusiasm into her voice, but couldn't muster much. Knowing Matt no longer got to do what he loved made her feel cheerless, and she didn't understand why.

"How is your old man anyway?" Ken asked.

Old man. She tried to envision Matt as a senior citizen with gray hair and wrinkles. No matter how he aged, she didn't think she could ever view him as anything other than the handsome, rugged man she'd married. "Actually, that's why I called."

"Oh?"

"Yeah, I was hoping maybe you could tell me why he left Oregon."

Another long pause. "He hasn't told you?"

"No. He limps now and walks with a cane. Do you know what happened to him?"

"Unfortunately, I do. But he should tell you about it, not me."

"That's not gonna happen, Ken. I've asked him about it twice and he keeps brushing it aside."

Silence filled the void for several heartbeats, as if Ken were thinking this over. "I was afraid of that. He won't accept help."

"Help for what?" she asked.

His voice lowered to a gruff rasp. "It was bad, Andie. Real bad. It was a relatively small brush fire last summer. Perhaps eighty acres. Matt and his crew were building a fire line and had moved up the hill. They were working hard and fast. If the fire made it over the ridge, it would have gone into big timber and out of control. Matt was determined to stop it, but not at the expense of his crew. No one blamed him for what happened."

Andie lowered her head and pressed her free hand to her forehead. She'd worked on enough wildfires to know the dangerous risks. "So what happened?"

"The wind changed suddenly, boxing Matt and one of his men into a small clearing. It was a fluke of nature no one could have seen coming. They deployed their fire shelters, but the heat of the fire was too intense. It killed one of his men. No one knows why Matt survived."

She released a shuddering breath, trying to absorb the ramifications of Ken's words like a sponge soaking up sand. It just wouldn't sink in. "Matt blames himself, doesn't he?"

"Yeah, but he won't talk about it, Andie. I know he's harboring tremendous guilt. He followed the ten standard wildfire-fighting orders and the eighteen watch-out situations, but he lost communication. Before he could rectify that, the winds changed. He did everything right, but it still happened so fast. I was hoping once he saw you, he might open up and let it go."

Ken went on to tell her about Matt's recovery. Four months. That's how long Matt had been in the Oregon Burn Center at Emmanuel Hospital in

Portland, recovering from second-and third-degree burns on his legs. Four months of excruciating pain.

"They didn't think he'd ever walk again, but he was determined. And once he sets his mind to do something, he does it," Ken said.

"Yeah, Matt was always like that." Her voice sounded strained.

"I know he was working with a physical therapist before he left for Nevada. He was pushing himself too hard, but he said he had to be ready to pass his work-capacity test for the new fire season."

"Why would he want to fight wildfires again?"

"It's what he does, what he's best at. I don't know if he can ever rehabilitate his leg for that kind of work again, but he's determined to try."

"He never would take no for an answer," Andie admitted.

In spite of her anger at Matt, she couldn't help feeling sorry for him. It was the risk every firefighter faced. Matt had been trained to deal with the danger, but how could he really prepare for the loss of one of the men under his command?

"It wasn't his fault, Andie."

She lifted her head, trying to still the shaking of her hands. "Why does he blame himself?"

"Because he was the crew boss. Because he survived."

Survivor's guilt.

"Oh!" She moaned and clenched her eyes closed,

imagining how she would feel if she lost one of her crew members in a wildfire. She'd be sick with anguish. They weren't just crew. They were friends. People you laughed with, ate and worked with every day. How could you tell their family that they wouldn't be coming home again?

"He almost died, Andie. By all rights, he shouldn't have survived. But you know Matt."

Yes, she knew Matt. Or at least, she used to know him. Now she wasn't so certain.

"Has he talked to you about the fire?" she asked.

Ken gave a harsh laugh. "Nope. Every time I brought it up, he shut me down. Almost losing his life changed him somehow. He insists he doesn't need to see a doctor. I visited him in the hospital several times. Once, he was delirious with pain and medication. All he talked about was seeing you and making things right with you again."

"Really?" Odd, since Matt had never called.

"Yeah, it seems he lost his way. All he would tell me was that the fire had changed his priorities. It made him see life differently. He told me how much he regretted giving up his family for his career, and he planned to make it right. More than anything, he wants your forgiveness, Andie."

Forgiveness. Something she didn't think she could give him. Now she understood why Matt had returned, but this was just a phase. Survivor's guilt. A backlash because he'd lived and his man hadn't. Eventually he would snap out of it and realize it was okay that he'd survived. Then he'd run off to some obscure destination to chase wildfires again. And where would that leave her and Davie?

Alone and brokenhearted. Again.

"He needs to speak with a specialist to help him deal with what happened," she said.

Ken released a whoosh of air. "I agree, but try telling that to Matt. He insists a physical therapist is all he needs."

Her stomach clenched tight. She longed to confide in Ken, but didn't dare. He might report back to Matt, and she refused to be held hostage by her husband simply because she felt compassion for him. "He's been gone from my life for over five years, Ken."

"Is it true you're still married?"

"In name only."

"Then there may still be a chance you two could work it out."

"No, I don't think that's possible anymore."

He paused. "I'm sorry to hear that. You two were always perfect for each other. Always so in love. Always interested in the same things."

"Except religion. I always believed in God, but Matt never did."

"Maybe that's what he needs now more than ever."

She hesitated. "You mean God?"

"Yeah—if ever he needed faith, it's now. Maybe you can help him see that."

No, no, no! She didn't want this responsibility. She didn't want to care about their marriage or Matt's eternal salvation. "Things are different now. We're basically strangers."

"So what are you gonna do?"

"I don't know. Because of our jobs, we have to work together. But we've both moved on with our lives. We've both changed. He left me, Ken. For a very long time."

"I know, and you have every right to be hurt. I told him many times that he should go see you and work things out. He said he'd tried to call you, but you never called back. He's different now, Andie. He's not the career-centered hotshot you once knew. And he needs you more than ever."

Again with the claim that he'd tried to call her. Andie had never received any voicemails from Matt. Not ever.

She gave a harsh laugh. "Are you advocating for him?"

"No, but I love him like a brother. He's always been there for me. He's bigger than life. An adrenaline junkie who thought he was invincible. After the fire, he learned that he's human, and it's made him realize what he lost the day he left you."

"I find that hard to believe."

"I think it's true. I hope you'll give him a second chance."

A second chance? No, she couldn't. Not with so

much to lose. She had to place Davie's well-being above anything else.

A loud buzzer and the sounds of voices in the background came from the phone receiver. "Look, Andie, I've got to go. But do me one favor. Just listen to Matt. If nothing else, try to be his friend. See if you can get him to open up. I fear he's like a powder keg waiting for a lighted match, but he's always trusted you. You may be his only hope. I'm deploying on a fire right now, but I'll check back with you in a few weeks."

"Okay, I'll let you go. Thanks and stay safe out there." She hung up the phone, staring at a dried splotch of coffee her range assistant had spilled on her desk the day before. Without thinking, she reached for a tissue, wet it in the water fountain, and scrubbed the smudge off her desk.

How could she be Matt's friend without caring for him? Without getting close to him again?

She couldn't. Wouldn't! No, he'd have to find some other way to deal with his grief. He could find God on his own. She had her son to think about now. There was just too much to lose this time.

But how could she turn her back on Matt? He was still her husband. The father of her child.

The love of her life.

Correction—ex-love of her life. She couldn't love him anymore. She didn't. She wouldn't.

She hated him. Hated him for how he'd hurt her. Didn't she?

She shook her head, the burn of tears and heartache more than she could stand. What was the use in denying it? She'd never stopped loving Matt, but she didn't like him very much right now. And how could she love a man she didn't like? He'd only break her heart again. How could she care so deeply for this man when she'd passed up the opportunity time and time again in his absence to build a healthy relationship with someone else? Every time Sue or one of Andie's friends tried to set her up on a blind date, she'd refused. In her profession, she'd met some very handsome, educated men who'd asked her out. And she'd refused every one.

Because they weren't Matt.

How could she turn her back on her husband when he needed her so much?

The answer came with clarity. She couldn't. But neither could she open her heart to being broken again. Once Matt reconciled his pain over what had happened during the wildfire, he could decide he didn't need her again and walk out. And where would that leave her and Davie?

As promised, Matt showed up on Andie's doorstep after work, toting a child-sized baseball bat, leather glove and a ball. As he rang the doorbell, he couldn't deny a buzz of excitement at having the opportunity to play with his son.

And to see Andie.

She'd gotten under his skin again. Like rushing into a wildfire, but something more intense than adrenaline. Seeing his family felt more like a drug he needed desperately. A consuming addiction he couldn't fight. He'd been anxious all day at work, watching the clock like a cat watches a mouse. Ready to pounce. By five o'clock, he felt as high-strung as a cougar in a cage. Then he'd been interrupted by Miles Ellsworth, the recreation staff engineer, wanting to discuss the impact of wildfires on the campgrounds. Making Matt late for his playtime with Davie.

Now Davie opened the door, grinning from ear to ear, a smudge of ketchup on his chin. "Hi, Dad. I didn't think you were coming."

Dad! Emotion flooded Matt with such intensity that he felt weak in the knees. To save his life, he couldn't explain what that one word did to him. He was a father, and he intended to be the best dad in the world from here on out. To honor Jim Lockrem.

He smiled wide. "Hi, son. Sorry, I got hung up at the office, but I wouldn't miss this for the world. You ready to play ball?"

Davie pushed the screen door wide and stepped back to let Matt inside. "Sure! But I have to finish dinner first."

Matt stepped into the living room, finding himself engulfed by the tantalizing aroma of cooking meat.

Andie sat at the kitchen table, holding a fork in midair. When she saw him, she came to her feet. "Have you eaten yet?"

He waved her off. "I'll get something later."

"Nonsense. We have plenty." She turned to the stove and scooped a large hamburger patty onto a bun, along with a pile of homemade fries and steamed broccoli.

At the table, Davie pulled out a chair for Matt and he set the baseball equipment by the door. He looped the handle of his cane over the back of the chair and sat down.

Davie wolfed down his burger while Andie placed a plate of food in front of Matt. He picked up his burger while she filled a tall glass with milk for him. She sat down and continued eating like nothing had happened. Davie pushed the bottle of ketchup and a plate of sliced Swiss and cheddar cheese toward him.

"Thanks." He smiled at his son, feeling out of sorts. Silence filled the room as he squirted ketchup on his burger and salted his broccoli.

Broccoli. Matt couldn't remember the last time he'd eaten a green vegetable or enjoyed a home-cooked meal. He hadn't been taking very good care of himself since the wildfire.

"How'd work go today?" Andie asked without looking up.

Such a casual question, but he stared at her, trying to absorb this whole situation. On the one hand, it felt so normal to be sitting here eating dinner with his family. On the other hand, a wide gulf stood between him and his wife, and he didn't know how to cross it.

"Fine. Just business."

Davie scraped his chair back from the table and raised his little hands in the air. "I'm done."

"Um, don't think so." Andie lifted her brows and stared at the two large spears of broccoli lying limp on Davie's plate.

"Ah, Mom. Do I have to eat it?" The boy groaned.

"Yes, you do."

"It's good for you. It'll make you a better baseball player." Matt picked up his fork and thrust a piece of broccoli into his own mouth before chewing with relish.

A look of repugnance crinkled Davie's nose. "How can you eat that stuff? It's yucky."

Matt chuckled. "Not if you put a little butter and salt on it. And maybe some cheese."

With a disgruntled frown, the boy sat down and reached for the plate of cheese slices. Both Matt and Andie continued eating, but they watched Davie as he broke a slice of cheddar into thin slivers and laid them on top of the broccoli. Then he salted the vegetable.

"Not too much," Andie cautioned.

The boy picked up his fork, jabbed the broccoli in a death thrust, then lifted it to his mouth. With an expression of agony, he popped it inside and chewed, then swallowed.

He looked at his dad and frowned. "The cheese doesn't help much, but it does make it a little bit better."

"One more and you're done," Andie said.

With a little sigh, Davie speared the last piece of broccoli and placed it in his mouth. Matt swallowed a laugh as he watched the pained expression on his son's face. The boy's cheeks bulged because he'd placed what should have been several bites into his mouth all at once.

With a huge swallow of milk, Davie washed down the offensive vegetable. Setting his glass aside, he laughed in victory. "I'm really done. Come on, Dad. We can go play now."

"I'm almost finished. Go get your baseball glove." Matt never knew having kids could be this much fun. As an only child, he'd never had any siblings or been close to his parents. He hoped to change that for Davie.

The boy raced down the hall to his room, leaving Matt alone with Andie. She showed a faint smile before eating her own broccoli.

"He's a good kid," Matt said for lack of something better to say.

"Yes, he is. But I doubt he'll ever like broccoli."

"That's normal. Most kids hate veggies. Maybe he'll like it when he's older."

"Maybe." She took a drink of milk. "How's your leg today?"

"Fine." He looked away so she wouldn't see the pain in his eyes. Few days passed when his leg didn't hurt like fire. While he'd watched Davie eat his dinner, Matt had forgotten his pain for several blissful minutes. Now it came back in full force.

He slid his hand beneath the table so he could rub his aching thigh muscle. Hopefully Andie didn't notice.

"How'd you hurt your leg, Matt?"

Andie's question took him off guard, and he dropped his fork to his plate with a clatter. "It was just an unfortunate accident."

"What kind of accident?" she pressed.

"It doesn't matter."

She set her fork aside and leaned her elbows on the table, looking him in the eye. "It matters to me. Tell me about it."

No! His mind screamed with anguish. Why wouldn't she let it drop? Speaking about what happened would only make him relive it in his mind. The smoke suffocating his lungs. The boiling heat of the fire as it melted his flesh. Jim's cries of pain that went on and on.

Jim Lockrem. Dead because of him. In the darkest part of each night, Jim's screams of agony still filled Matt's ears until he sobbed with anguish.

Even now, Matt couldn't figure out why he'd survived. He would bear the scars on his legs for the rest of his life.

A constant reminder of what he'd done.

Matt clenched his eyes closed, wishing he could go back in time and change things somehow. Wishing he could forget.

"I was injured in a brush fire." He barely got the words out around the lump in his throat.

"What happened?"

"I got burned and they took me to the hospital. That's it." He scraped his chair back from the table and gripped his cane like a lifeline as he stood.

She glanced at his half-eaten burger. "You haven't finished eating."

"I'm not really hungry. You ready to go, Davie?"

"Almost," the boy called.

"Matt." Andie also stood, her eyes filled with the one thing he just could not accept from her. Pity.

"Don't, Andie. Just let it go. I'm dealing with it the best way I can. I don't want to talk about it." He hobbled to the door, refusing to look at her. Refusing to let her see the torment in his eyes. If he let down his guard now, he'd end up like a puddle of water on the living room floor. And he couldn't do that. Not if he wanted to keep his sanity.

Davie came running, wearing a jacket, baseball cap and his leather glove. "I'm ready."

Matt wrenched the door open a bit too hard before picking up the baseball bat. Ignoring the dishes, Andie grabbed a sweater from the hall closet and followed them outside, sitting on the front porch steps while Matt played with Davie in the front yard. Matt couldn't help wondering if she were making sure he didn't kidnap the boy, or if she just wanted to watch them have fun.

"The daylight will be gone soon. Let's try some practice throws to warm up," Matt said.

Davie stood back, waiting expectantly.

"Hold your hands up, not down by your sides. You want to be ready when the ball comes toward you."

The boy lifted his arms, elbows bent. Matt tossed the ball and Davie tried to catch it, dropped it, then scrambled after it on the damp grass.

"Great effort, son." Matt was glad his boy wasn't afraid of the ball. Davie had lots of potential.

Again and again, they threw the ball back and forth to each other. Davie caught it only once, but he had some near misses. He was getting better.

"How about if I pitch to you now?" Matt called.

"Yeah. I'm much better at hitting the ball. Coach says I'm a real slugger."

Matt chuckled, then stared in surprise as Davie rubbed dirt onto his hands, then picked up the bat and tapped it against his sneaker. Matt tried not to laugh at the ritual, but failed miserably. "Where'd you learn that?"

Davie bent his legs and squatted slightly, holding the bat aloft as he waited for the pitch. "I saw it on TV. All the pros do it. Mom and I like to watch baseball together. She says I can never chew tobacco and spit, though."

Thank goodness.

Matt glanced at Andie, who had wrapped her arms around herself and leaned forward on the top step of the porch. He caught a glint of amusement in her eyes.

"You don't need to chew tobacco and spit to be a great baseball player. In fact, I'd prefer it if you didn't do those things. Tobacco isn't good for you, and spitting is rude." Matt caught a nod of approval from Andie.

"I won't, Dad. I already promised Mom. Come on. Pitch."

Matt tossed the ball gently and soon learned that Davie meant what he said. The little boy swung the bat hard, hitting the ball dead-on with a loud crack that sent it flying across the hedge into the neighbor's yard.

"Wow! You weren't kidding, were you? You can really hit."

"Yep! I'll get it." Davie dropped the bat and trotted off to retrieve the ball.

Matt glanced at Andie, who watched him quietly. He hobbled closer to chat with her for a moment. "You didn't tell me how good he is for his age. He's amazing."

She shrugged. "He takes after his father. Why are you so surprised by his natural athletic ability?"

"I couldn't hit the ball like that when I was almost six years old. By the time Davie's out of high school, he'll be on a full-ride scholarship to any university in the nation."

Finally she cracked a wide smile. "I sure hope so."

"Ah, there you are." He smiled back.

"What do you mean?"

"I knew you could remember how to smile."

The smile dropped from her face like stone. "I haven't had a lot of reasons to smile lately."

Matt inclined his chin toward Davie. "I think that boy is a pretty good reason to smile, sweetheart. You've done a great job with him."

She opened her mouth to say something, but Davie returned, flushed and gasping for breath.

"I figure that was a home run," the boy said happily.

Matt tugged on the brim of Davie's ball cap. "I figure you're right. Good job, hotshot."

Beaming at his father's praise, Davie took up the bat again. They continued to play ball with Davie hitting almost every pitch Matt tossed at him, then chasing after the ball while Matt and Andie made small talk.

Within an hour, Matt could take no more. The intense pain in his thigh made it difficult to walk. "It's too dark. We better quit for tonight."

"Aw, do you have to go?" Davie whined.

"I'm afraid so." Matt grit his teeth to keep from

showing the agony he felt as he hobbled over to his truck.

Andie stood on the porch watching him go. She didn't return his wave, able to hear his conversation with their son.

"You'll come back tomorrow, won't you?" Davie asked.

Matt looked up at Andie. The wind ruffled her long hair, her expression closed off. It used to be so easy to talk to her. To read on her face what she was thinking. Now he saw nothing there but cold reservation. Both of them were harboring their own angst. If only he could cross the divide between them. "If it's okay with your mom."

Davie whirled around to look at his mother and yelled at the top of his lungs. "Is it okay if Dad comes over to play again tomorrow, Mom?"

She hesitated and Matt held his breath, waiting. He couldn't believe he wanted to come play games with a five-year-old boy, but he couldn't get enough of his little son. Or Andie. How he wished he didn't have to go home to his lonely apartment.

"Yes," Andie said before turning away.

Matt let out a *whoosh* of air, unable to deny a feeling of euphoria. It dimmed the pain in his leg and in his heart.

Tomorrow. He'd come back and visit his son again. And Andie. The woman he loved.

Chapter Six

True to his word, Matt showed up again the next evening, and the next. The days became a whirlwind of work and evening play with Davie. Rain or shine, Matt spent every minute teaching Davie to catch a baseball and slide into home plate.

Andie tried to broach the subject of the wildfire again, but Matt shut her down with a stern look. He didn't want to confide in her and she couldn't blame him. Without him saying so, she knew he must feel culpable for losing his crewman. She feared the guilt might be eating him up inside. And then she wondered why she cared. Matt wasn't the same anymore, but neither was Andie. Over the years, they'd grown apart and might never feel comfortable around each other again. They harbored too much hurt, anger and resentment.

Or at least she did. She couldn't figure out Matt's motives. To save her life, she just could not believe him when he said he regretted leaving her. Too many years had gone by. They'd both moved on with their lives.

Or had they? Somehow she felt stunted in life, as though she couldn't really move on until she resolved the issue of her marriage to Matt.

By Friday afternoon, Andie felt jittery as she drove to the Forest Supervisor's office for a fire meeting with Matt and the other district rangers. She parked beside the flagpole and shut off the motor, sitting quietly for several moments to gain her composure. Her boss and colleagues would be present. As the only woman ranger on the forest, she needed to appear professional and confident. Her personal feelings for Matt had no place in this meeting.

She looked in the rearview mirror to ensure strands of hair hadn't come loose from the clip she'd pulled it up into at the back of her head. Stepping out of her car, she smoothed her spruce-green pants and checked her ranger shirt to make sure she hadn't spilled any lunch on it. With her laptop and several files held securely in her arms, she made her way up the sidewalk and into the main foyer of the redbrick building.

"Hi, Andie." Craig Spencer, the ranger from the Bridgeport District, greeted her.

"How you doing, Craig?"

"Good." He leaned closer and whispered for her ears alone. "I'm eager to hear the fire plan from our new FCO. Have you met him yet?"

She bit back a hard cough. "Yes, I've met him."

"And what do you think of him?"

Oh, boy. That opened the corral gate. But Andie didn't want her colleagues to know about her personal relationship with Matt. Her work should stand on its own merits, not her marriage. "I think he's highly qualified for the position."

Okay, that was true enough. With his training and background experience, no one knew wildfire fighting better than Matt. Even in her anger, she couldn't help feeling proud of his accomplishments.

They gathered around the wide table in the conference room to await the other attendees. Sherry, the administrative assistant, urged them to help themselves to pastries, coffee and drinks. Andie chose a bottle of water and sat down to wait. Within minutes, the room filled with people. She and Miriam Christensen, the Watershed, Soils and Range staff officer, were the only women in the room. More than ever, Andie felt the pressure to perform well and was determined not to fail.

Cal Hinkle came in and greeted them each with a handshake. He made chitchat while the other rangers milled around the coffeepot. Then he took his seat at the front of the room.

Andie was deep in conversation with Miriam when Matt walked in. Without looking up, Andie sensed his presence. Like radar. As she turned her head and saw him talking with Craig, she became conscious of him not as an enemy, but as a very handsome man.

Her man.

A twinge of desire settled in her chest. She couldn't help remembering the strong gentleness of his arms around her or the scent of his warm skin. It'd been a long time, and she mourned the loss of the closeness they'd once shared.

No, he wasn't her man anymore. And yet, as long as they were married and shared a child, she couldn't help feeling possessive.

Cal cleared his voice, signaling it was time to get down to business. "We have a number of new people I'd like to welcome. Matt Cutter has joined our team as the new FCO and brings with him a wealth of knowledge I think we'll soon come to appreciate."

Matt nodded, his eyes aglow with appreciation.

"Andie Foster is the new ranger over Enlo District, and Tim Bellows is the new ranger over Austin District. Both highly qualified. We're glad to have you on our team. Welcome to you all." Cal smiled warmly at each newcomer.

Andie nodded, conscious of Matt's gaze resting on her. It seemed no one else was in the room, just her and Matt. She forced herself to concentrate on what the S.O. was saying.

"…and I think you're all highly aware that we're having a dry winter and expect a hot summer. That means wildfire. I'm going to turn the floor over to Matt now. He's designed a plan to help us work more efficiently together and communicate better. Matt?"

Cal looked at Matt with expectation as he sat down.

Matt braced his hands on the table and rose, using his cane to hobble over to a PowerPoint projector. Knowing what he'd been through in the wildfire, Andie's heart ached with every step he took.

Using a remote clicker, Matt gave a presentation on a new communication structure and heavy-machinery sharing amongst the various districts. By the time he was finished, Andie was impressed by his knowledge of the forest and the various needs of each ranger district. She had also studied the requirements of her district and felt concerned by a few of his proposals.

"Are there any questions?" he asked.

She raised her hand. "Did I notice correctly that you plan to station two pumper trucks in Bridgeport?"

He nodded. "Yes. There's no doubt we don't have enough cats and pumpers to go around, but I'd like to station two pumpers in Bridgeport during the high-danger season."

She tried not to bristle at Matt, but couldn't help questioning his logic. "I mean no disrespect to Craig, but Bridgeport is over two hundred miles away from Enlo. What are we supposed to do until the pumper trucks can reach us during a fire? We tend to have more fires, and we have heavier timber than Bridgeport."

Matt met her eyes, speaking in a reasonable tone. "I took that into account, but you already have several pumpers, while Bridgeport only has one. Stationing the two extra pumpers in Enlo would be too far away from Bridgeport to respond adequately to wildfires there."

Andie didn't like this. She glanced at Cal to see his expression. He had the last word on the subject.

"I'm afraid I'll have to side with Matt on this issue, Andie. We really need the extra pumpers in Bridgeport."

Other issues weighed on her mind, too. She tried to tell herself her objections had nothing to do with Matt being her estranged husband. She was just doing her job, looking out for her district. But worrying about Matt had made her grouchy.

She met Matt and Cal's gazes without blinking, telling herself she must remain professional. "I'm also concerned about the long-term considerations of where to build an adequate facility to house pumpers and take care of our equipment. I'd rather see that facility built in Enlo, not in Reno."

Matt shook his head. "I disagree. Reno is larger and a good location to house the equipment. During fire season, we can move the trucks and station them anywhere on the forest."

Andie bit her tongue, forcing herself to take two breaths before responding. She didn't get the chance.

Cal's brows drew together in a thoughtful frown. "Um, I'm afraid I'll have to agree with Andie on this one, Matt. I think Enlo would be an ideal location to build the facility. Hopefully we'll get more funding to house a few more pumper trucks in Reno also."

Andie sat back, pleased to have gotten her way on one issue. When she looked at Matt, she couldn't help flashing a smile of triumph. Matt took her completely off guard when he winked at her, and her smile faded just as quickly. She was feeling territorial and competitive, but that didn't disrupt his good humor. She felt childish for letting her personal feelings get in the way of her work and promised herself not to do it again. Matt knew what he was doing, and so did she. Stationing the pumpers in Bridgeport was simply a business decision, nothing more. It wasn't personal.

The meeting continued with discussions about the fire school Matt had scheduled to host in early May to train summer wildfire fighters. Matt made several assignments, expecting each ranger to teach a specific technique in dealing with fighting wildfire.

"Andie, I understand you qualify as a Division Group Supervisor and passed your arduous physical. Would you be able to teach fire-line construction?" Matt asked.

The other rangers looked at her expectantly. She had an excellent pumper crew on her district and would prefer teaching that, but it wasn't reasonable to argue this time. "Sure. I can do that."

The meeting soon ended and Andie breathed a sigh of relief. It hadn't been easy, but she'd proven to herself that she could work with Matt with a minimum of fallout.

"Thanks for coming, everyone. Have a safe trip home." Cal stood and paused. "Matt and Andie, would you remain behind for a few minutes? I need to speak with you briefly."

Andie felt her throat sink to her feet. Maybe things hadn't gone as well as she thought.

The room soon emptied, leaving Andie alone with Matt and Cal. Matt remained where he'd been sitting the entire meeting, and Andie sensed his leg must be hurting him. A blaze of sympathy tore through her when she considered that he must be living with severe chronic pain. How did he do it every day without complaining?

Cal and Andie took their seats.

"What's up?" Matt opened the discussion by leaning forward and resting his elbows on the table.

Cal's chair creaked as he sat back and looked at them, his forehead furrowed with concern. "It may be nothing, but I sense some hostility between you two. There's no easy way to say this, but do you two have a problem working together?"

Oh, boy. Andie's mouth dropped open in surprise, but Matt's face remained passive. Unlike Andie, he'd always been good at hiding his emotions. Under the circumstances, Andie figured they'd done quite well today. She didn't think she'd been rude in questioning Matt's judgment, but perhaps her demeanor and harsher tone of voice had given her away.

Matt spoke first. "No, sir, I have no problem at all working with Andie. In fact, I count myself lucky to be able to work with such a qualified ranger. I have nothing but respect for her."

Wow! What could Andie say to that? Likewise, she believed Matt was perfect for the job of FCO. Just not on this national forest. Not here with her. But she had to get along.

"I agree that I have no problem working with Matt." She looked at her husband. "I apologize if I sounded rude when I questioned your judgment earlier. I intended no harm. I know you're looking after the best interests of the entire forest."

He flashed her a crooked smile. "No offense taken. You were also just doing your job."

"I agree," Cal said. "Maybe I'm overreacting, but I sensed an undercurrent here that perhaps doesn't exist. Have you two met before you accepted your new assignments here?"

Andie bit her bottom lip. Cal didn't know they were married because Andie went by her maiden name.

"Yes…we first met long ago in college," she said.

Okay, it was the truth, although she omitted the part about getting married and having a child.

"Ah, then you do know each other."

Matt nodded. "Yes, quite well."

"Then I'm not going to worry about it. Our forest is lucky to have you both, and I'll trust that you'll get along and work together for the greater good."

"Yes, sir," Matt said.

"Absolutely," Andie agreed.

Cal stood. "Good, then. I'll let you get back to work. Thanks for staying behind to have this chat."

A rush of relief fell over Andie. She tried to swallow, but her throat had a lump in it the size of Kansas. The room seemed to close in on her. She had to get out of here. Now.

Because of his leg, Matt moved more slowly. Andie stood and shook Cal's hand, then made a hasty retreat. She planned to take Davie to the movies tonight with Sue and Brett. Matt wasn't coming over to practice baseball with Davie, and she looked forward to the reprieve. She needed time to clear her head and think.

She needed time away from her husband.

At the movie, Andie went with Brett to get seats while Sue and Davie bought popcorn. Andie led the way up the dimly lit stairs, followed by Brett, who carried little Rose.

"Is this okay?" She indicated some rocking seats midway up the theater.

"Yeah, Davie should like this."

She chuckled. "He'd have me go all the way up to the top if I would. That boy is just like his father. Always wants the biggest, fastest, highest possible."

Brett sat in the aisle seat while Andie moved over two seats so that Sue could sit next to her husband, with Davie beside Andie. "Sounds like Matt's an adrenaline junky."

Andie crossed her legs and rested back in her chair. "He used to be, although I think the last wildfire he was on may have cured him of that."

"You mean the one that injured his leg? Sue mentioned it to me."

"Uh-huh. He won't talk about it, but I've heard a few things that make me wonder what happened. I know it was serious enough to take the life of one of his crew members and nearly kill him."

Brett shifted the baby in his lap and handed her a bottle. "Andie, what happened to make Matt leave?"

"Sue didn't tell you?"

He smiled with compassion. "Yeah, she told me, but I'd like to hear your version."

She glanced at him, then stared at the advertisements flashing across the wide movie screen. She spoke low so other people around them wouldn't overhear. "We had a fight. A bad one."

"What about?"

She released a deep sigh. "He'd put in on a hot-shot job without my knowledge. When he got the job, he wanted me to just pick up and move with him to Oregon. I knew what it would lead to. Constant absences as he deployed on highly dangerous jobs."

"And?"

She squirmed. "And I told him no, I wouldn't go."

"So he left you?"

"Not exactly. I told him to leave, and he did."

"Is that what you really wanted? For him to leave?"

She brushed a strand of hair away from her eyes, an excuse to absorb the tears beading in the corners of her eyes. Hopefully the dim theater hid her expression. "Of course not. He should have known that. I still can't believe he left without saying goodbye. Without talking it over some more."

"How could he have known if you didn't tell him?"

She realized the part she'd played in Matt leaving, and it wasn't pretty. Knowing she was partly to blame in their separation didn't make his return any easier. She thought she'd sorted all of this out. Apparently not. Old feelings of longing came crashing down on her, leaving her feeling more bereft and lonely inside. It'd been so easy to blame Matt for the rift in their marriage. To excuse her own part in his leaving. But if she were honest, she had to admit she'd pushed him away. She could have called or gone to see him, to say she didn't really mean it. And if her marriage was the most important thing to her, she should have gone with him, knowing it meant so much to him. Instead, she'd waited for him to make the first move. Finally he had, and still she pushed him away.

"It's not too late, you know?" Brett interrupted her thoughts.

"It's been more than five years, Brett."

"So? He's here now, you're here, you're still married and you created a beautiful little boy together. Matt obviously wants to make things right again. He made the first move to make things right. So what's stopping you from telling him you never wanted him to leave?"

Fear! Distrust! She wanted to scream.

What if Matt changed his mind and decided to leave again? She couldn't take that hurt and rejection all over. It was too late for her and Matt. But Davie adored his father. If Matt left again, her son would be devastated no matter what she did.

So would she.

So what should she do? Sue would tell her to avoid Matt at all costs, but that would do Davie no good.

Andie thought of confiding in God, but she

didn't know how anymore. It'd been so long since she'd prayed or let God into her life. So long since she'd felt the Comforter near. She'd blamed both Matt and God for the loss of her marriage. She'd blamed them for every problem and sadness in her life. Her anger had caused her to lose her trust in the Lord and in humanity. It'd taken the birth of her son to bring her joy again, and even that event had been bittersweet, knowing Matt wasn't there to share it with her.

"Are you telling me I should make a go of my marriage to Matt?" she asked.

"I'm not telling you anything. I'm just suggesting that you might give Matt a second chance." Brett reached across the seats and squeezed her hand.

"Did he talk to you?"

"No, but he looks at you like a lovesick puppy dog."

Andie laughed. The lovestruck look Brett claimed to see written across Matt's face could be nothing more than indigestion.

"You're a romantic, Brett." Dear, gentle Brett. A large man filled with a big heart.

He shrugged one shoulder. "Guilty as accused. But don't tell Sue. She doesn't think I have a romantic bone in my body."

Sue appeared at the bottom of the theater, holding Davie's hand as they climbed the stairs up to their seats.

With his wife near, Brett clamped his mouth

closed on this subject. Andie didn't blame him. The topic of Matt made Susan furious. Andie was the eldest, but she'd come to depend on her baby sister since Matt had left. Sue meant well.

"What candy did you choose, champ?" Brett rested a large hand on Davie's shoulder as the boy squeezed past his knees to reach his seat beside Andie.

"Goobers." Davie held the package up for Brett's inspection.

"Give me that. I want it." When Brett made a playful grab for the candy, Davie squealed and dashed toward his mother.

Andie laughed as they settled down to watch the movie, a children's flick that would undoubtedly put Brett to sleep within ten minutes.

As the movie commenced, she couldn't help thinking Matt would love to be here with them. Discovering he was a father had changed him so much. He seemed such a natural dad with Davie. She longed to help Matt find peace of mind over what had happened on the wildfire, and yet that effort seemed like the blind leading the blind.

Until she could accept God back into her life again, she realized she wouldn't be able to heal or forgive Matt. Or herself. There would be no peace in her heart.

Chapter Seven

On Saturday, Andie had to do some quick maneuvering on the bleachers so Matt wouldn't sit beside her during Davie's T-ball game. She climbed up high where it would be difficult for Matt to follow on his bad leg. To her horror, her son came racing over just before the game started and greeted Matt at the top of his lungs.

"Hi, Dad. You made it. Hey, Brian! This is my dad. I told you I had a dad. This is him." Davie pointed at Matt and everyone in the bleachers turned to stare.

Brian nodded, not looking too impressed.

Andie's face burned with embarrassment as everyone then turned to look at her. Friends and associates. People from work and church. She could see the questions in their eyes as they whispered together about this revelation. Had she divorced Matt? Or conceived her son out of wedlock?

Turning away, she fumed silently to herself. Let

them wonder. She didn't care what people thought. She owed them no explanation. This wasn't Matt's fault, but she wished he hadn't come today.

And then she felt guilty. Matt sat on the bottom bleacher, his back straight, smiling at his son. He looked lonely down there, yet he didn't seem to mind. She should go down and sit with him. She should be more charitable.

"You don't look happy about Davie's announcement. You okay?" Sue scooted in beside Andie, with little Rose and a fat diaper bag in her arms. The baby wore a warm cap and coat against the chilly breeze, though the sky above showed nothing but blue.

"Yeah, I'm just dandy." Andie stared at Matt's broad back as he leaned his cane against his leg. His presence here today felt like a sharp sliver in her foot. A painful annoyance.

"I didn't know you were divorced." Brian Phelps's mother, Claudia, turned around and leaned toward Andie. "I thought you were a widow."

Andie met the woman's stare with cool disdain. Claudia taught Sunday school at church and was also the wife of Ted Phelps, the forest engineer. "I'm not a widow."

"Then you're still married? I had no idea Matt Cutter was your husband." Claudia's nasal voice sounded loud enough for many people around them to hear.

It was on the edge of Andie's tongue to deny it.

But why? She'd married the right man at the right time in the right place. She'd done nothing wrong. "Yes, we're married."

A Cheshire cat grin spread across Claudia's face. "How interesting."

The woman turned back around and Andie felt a sinking feeling of dread. Ted worked in the S.O.'s office. Andie wondered how long it would take for the Forest Supervisor to find out she and Matt were married. How could she explain to her boss that she and Matt were married in name only and no longer lived together? Would it matter?

Matt tossed a worried glance her way, and she realized he'd also heard Claudia's comments. No doubt he didn't want trouble, either. If they were lucky, the issue wouldn't come up again.

"The old biddy. She should mind her own business," Sue whispered beneath her breath.

Andie squeezed her sister's hand before reaching to take Rose into her arms. For several moments, she kissed and snuggled the baby. How she wished she could have more children. Having Sue here to offer quiet support brought Andie more comfort than she could say. Even Sue's dislike of Matt was only because Sue loved and wanted to protect Andie. Andie felt lucky to have a sister like Sue.

They watched the game for some time, cheering when one of the boys on Davie's team stole a base. Then they yelled their displeasure when the ref made a bad call.

And then Andie got the startle of her life. The best player on the other team hit a long ball, and Davie caught it in midair.

"Yer out!" the umpire called as he dragged his thumb toward the dugouts.

Andie cheered her head off. Happy pleasure suffused her entire body. Davie had gotten an out. He'd caught the ball. Because his daddy had been practicing with him for two weeks.

Matt stood on his wobbly leg, his face beaming a wide smile. He clapped his hands and turned to look at her. She couldn't help returning his smile. For the first time since he'd become aware that he had a son, Andie shared something special with him. They were both Davie's parents and buoyantly pleased with their little boy's accomplishment.

Davie's team won by two points. Following the game, Davie ran immediately to his father, throwing his little arms around Matt's neck and hugging tight. "I did it, Dad. Did you see me?"

"I did, son. You were great."

Andie couldn't help feeling a bit snubbed. In the past, it had always been her that Davie ran to. And yet, she couldn't begrudge Matt this honor.

"Hey, Mom! Aunt Sue! Did you see me catch that ball?" Davie waved at them.

"Yes, we saw you. Well done."

"I'm out of here. I'd rather not make chitchat with your rotten husband." Sue spoke to Andie as she gathered Rose into her arms and stepped past on the bleachers.

"See you tomorrow." Andie kissed her sister on the cheek, then went to join Davie and Matt.

"I did just like you told me and kept my eye on the ball," Davie said to his father.

"I know. You tried very hard. And then you got a home run. You were great today."

Oh, no. Andie inhaled sharply. All this time, she'd been worried about Davie falling in love with his daddy. But when she looked at Matt and saw the warm devotion glittering in his eyes, she realized she hadn't contemplated Matt loving Davie. Yeah, most parents loved their kids. But for a long time, she had been the focus of Davie's life. Now someone else in this world adored her son and would do anything for him. This seemed to bring Matt and Andie even closer. Their son was a bond they shared with no one else and could not deny.

"You want to come to church with us tomorrow?" Davie asked Matt.

"Davie, no. Your dad doesn't go to church." Her son seemed to have developed a habit of inviting Matt to anything and everything in their life.

"Actually, I'd like that." Matt looked at her with deep honesty.

"You would?" How many shocks could she absorb?

"Yes, I would."

How could she tell her husband that she felt unworthy of God? She hadn't really lost her faith in the Lord, but somehow over the past few years, she'd become apathetic. God hadn't been there for her when Matt left and Davie was born, nor when she'd gotten her new promotion. As a busy career woman, she'd let life crowd out the Lord. It'd been so long since she'd prayed with earnestness. But she needed to teach Davie about God. There might come a day when her son needed Him in his life, and if she didn't teach Davie, who would? People who didn't believe in the Lord?

"But you never used to believe in God. Or at least you had no use for Him. I always had to go to church alone when we were…" She left that thought hanging.

"That's changed," Matt said.

Hmm. Andie had missed quite a bit of church. She definitely believed in God, but she figured she couldn't harbor hate in her heart toward her husband and still have room for the Lord. She wasn't sure she was ready to let it go.

"We'll see you there, then. Come on, Davie. We need to get home." She took the boy by the hand.

"But what about pizza? You promised we'd get pizza after the game."

Andie almost groaned out loud. How she wished Davie had forgotten about that. Now he'd probably invite Matt along, and she didn't want to appear rude when she told him no.

"You two have fun," Matt said.

"You can come with us, can't he, Mom?"

Yep, just as she'd predicted. She shifted her weight, trying to think of a polite way to say no.

"Sorry, hotshot, but I can't." Matt smiled down at Davie.

"Ah, how come?"

"I've got work to do. But maybe another time, okay?"

"Okay," Davie grumbled.

Andie met Matt's gaze, realizing he'd made this easier on her. Worse than inviting him along for dinner, she now felt grateful to him. She shouldn't feel grumpy about it, but she'd been on her own with Davie for so long. She admitted silently to herself that she felt threatened by Matt. She didn't like competing for her son's affection.

Oh, that was silly. Matt was Davie's father. She shouldn't begrudge the two of them spending time together and having a good time. She was being foolish.

Matt smiled and winked at her. "See you two later."

Turning, he hobbled off, and a feeling of compassion almost overwhelmed Andie. Watching her previously strong husband now crippled and stumbling with a cane almost broke her heart. It made her want to call him back and ask him to eat pizza and laugh with them. But she didn't want to. She didn't want this man back in her life, attending

Davie's T-ball games. How could she remain angry at Matt while feeling grateful to him?

Without loving him?

She couldn't. And that bothered her most of all. She refused to love any man. Ever again.

Matt locked his truck, then turned and faced the redbrick church house. The wide double doors beckoned to him, the sounds of two little girls' laughter filling the air as they raced ahead of their mother. They each wore a dainty sweater that matched their blue dresses. The warm March weather had brought forth a plethora of tulips, daffodils and green sprouts in the flower beds lining the building.

"Children, it's time to be reverent," the mother called to them.

They stood holding the door wide while she carried a toddler and a bag of books inside.

Matt hesitated, feeling nervous and out of place. An odd emotion for him. No matter the situation, he'd always been confident and in control. But not in church and not since the wildfire. Now the only thing he felt certain of was his desire to be a better husband and father and earn Andie's love again.

In the mass of flame and smoke, he'd prayed for the first time in his life. Survival was a natural instinct. He'd lived and he couldn't understand why he'd been pulled to safety while Jim had died. In his darkest hour of pain, Matt had promised the

Lord he'd make everything right again, with Andie and with his faith. He just didn't know how to go about it. He'd never believed in God, but a miracle had been worked on his behalf and now he found himself wanting to believe. Andie might not give him a second chance, but he had to try.

He didn't know anyone at church. Maybe Andie and Davie were inside already. But that wouldn't help. Andie obviously wanted as little to do with Matt as possible. Still, he had to try.

He limped down the sidewalk edging the green lawn, determined to go inside. Determined to be a better man. His promise to God wasn't contingent upon feeling comfortable in a new congregation. He wasn't here to win a popularity contest, but to be near his family and learn about the Lord. Then he could decide if he believed or not.

Matt lengthened his stride, glad the physical therapy and exercises were strengthening his legs. In the main foyer, he found himself surrounded by happy people greeting one another. Parents bustled their children into the chapel. Two women chatted together as they made last-minute arrangements for an upcoming activity. The air smelled of furniture polish, the gray carpets showing vacuum streaks from a recent cleaning.

Matt followed the soft sounds of organ music coming from the chapel. Inside, an elderly woman smiled and nodded at him, but didn't speak as she sat down.

Matt's gaze automatically scanned the pews, looking for Andie and Davie, or another friendly face. There they were, his wife and son. Sitting toward the front with Sue and a man Matt assumed must be Brett. They sat with their backs to him, but Matt recognized the slim column of Andie's graceful neck. She'd pulled her hair up in loose curls and wore a white dress with pink rosebuds edging the dainty collar. She looked so beautiful today.

Davie sat between Andie and Sue, playing with Sue's baby daughter. The boy saw Matt and waved.

"Hi, Dad!"

Matt tightened his lips. His son certainly was not a quiet child. Several people turned to look at him and he shifted his weight on the cane, feeling uncomfortable with this new attention. Not because he was embarrassed to be Davie's father, but because he knew his presence upset Andie.

She turned her head and looked at him from over her shoulder, her eyes filled with alarm. Susan glared for several seconds, then turned around and completely ignored him. Her husband leaned near, listening as she whispered something to him. From her severe expression, Matt could tell she spoke harsh words. The man glanced at Matt, frowned, then responded to Sue. She shook her head, her shoulders stiff. No doubt they were discussing him.

The black sheep returned to the flock.

What should Matt do? He couldn't stand here all day. His leg pounded like a bass drum, and the service would begin soon. He needed to find a place to sit.

He longed to join his family, but the perturbed glint in Andie's eyes warned him to stay away. It seemed like everyone in the chapel was staring at him with disapproval. His wife and sister-in-law hated him. This was a mistake.

He didn't belong here.

As he turned to leave, Sue's husband stood and walked down the aisle to greet him. Dressed in a dark suit with a white shirt and tie, the man held out his hand, and Matt met his gaze with surprise.

"Hi, Matt. I'm Brett Osborn, Sue's husband. I believe we're brothers-in-law."

Although Matt stood six feet and three inches, Brett towered over him with beefy arms and hands that spoke of great strength. Matt shook Brett's hand, stunned by his warm greeting. "I guess so."

"Won't you come and sit with your family?" Brett stood back, holding an arm out to indicate he expected Matt to precede him up the aisle.

"I don't think that's such a good idea." Out of his peripheral vision, Matt saw Andie facing forward and wrestling with Davie to get him to do the same.

Brett lowered his head and whispered for Matt's ears alone. "You're not gonna let those two women scare you off, are you? Whether she admits it or not, Andie needs you as much as Davie does. Badly. Come on."

Laughter filled Brett's eyes, and Matt realized he had an ally. As he accompanied Brett up the aisle, Matt hoped he didn't regret this later on.

Andie threw him a scowl and forced Sue and the children to scoot down to make room for him on the bench. Matt tried to slide into his seat, but he wasn't limber enough and ended up bumping against Andie.

"Sorry," he murmured.

She heaved a sigh of resignation, staring at the pulpit.

Davie crossed in front of his mother and came to sit beside Matt, which forced another bout of scooting down to make more room. "Hi, Daddy."

"Hi, sweetheart." Matt pulled his son up onto his lap and kissed his forehead. It felt good to be wanted by someone. He'd never been a sentimental man, but now he held Davie to him like a lifeline. He loved this child more than anything, except for Andie. If only she could see into his heart and understand how sorry he was for hurting her. How badly he wished she'd forgive him and grant him a second chance.

As the meeting began, Matt heard Sue's impatient huff and then another harsh whisper to her husband. "Why did you invite him, Brett? He's not part of our family anymore. He's nothing but trouble."

Brett's calm response reassured Matt. "He's

a child of God, just like you and me. And he's Davie's father. That makes him part of our family forever."

"But he's not..." Sue's voice faded as she leaned closer to her husband's ear.

Brett put his arm around Sue's shoulders and gave her a gentle squeeze, his voice a quiet murmur. "Show a little Christian compassion, honey."

That won Brett an angry glare from Sue. She shrugged his arm away on the pretense of reaching for the baby.

But what about Andie? She was Matt's wife; she and Davie were his entire world now. If she refused to accept Matt, he was all alone, no matter how hard Brett tried to advocate on his behalf. Once again, Matt realized with perfect clarity and great regret how Andie must have felt when he'd left her all those years ago. He couldn't blame her for being distant and angry.

Andie stared straight ahead, her face void of expression. But he knew from her tensed shoulders that she was perturbed. It would take a miracle for her to forgive him, but that's what he needed if he were to ever be whole again.

Her forgiveness.

Chapter Eight

"We're having roast beef dinner over at Aunt Sue's house. You're coming, aren't you?" Davie looked up at Matt, his face filled with hope.

They stood in the front foyer of the church following Sunday school. Except for Sue's hateful glower and Andie's occasional looks of frustration, Matt had thoroughly enjoyed the lessons he'd learned today. Though he hadn't participated in the discussion, he'd felt exquisite peace as he'd listened to a talk about the Savior and the Atonement. He wasn't sure what he believed yet, but he couldn't explain how he felt. A quiet, warm feeling inside. Even Sue didn't bother him as he sat beside Andie, breathing in the sweet fragrance of her shampoo.

"Davie, remember I asked you to check with me first before inviting people over?" Andie lifted her brows at her son.

"But I didn't think that meant Dad. He's not people. He's family."

An expression of aggravation covered Andie's face.

"Of course your dad's invited to dinner," Brett chimed in.

Matt's eyes widened and Sue jabbed her husband with her elbow, her face tight with anger.

"Here's our address and phone numbers." Brett ignored his wife and handed Matt a piece of paper with the info scrawled across it.

The two women stared at Brett like he'd just grown a tail and horns.

"Thanks, but I can't make it." Matt shook his head, wanting nothing more than to sit down and eat dinner with Andie and Davie.

He wouldn't mind spending time getting to know Brett, either, but Sue was a different story. He'd grown weary of her hateful looks and longed to prop up his leg with an ice pack. He dreaded the exercises awaiting him and thought maybe he'd give himself a day off, to rest his leg.

"Nonsense. We won't take no for an answer," Brett said.

"Brett! He said he's busy," Sue warned.

"Aw, Mom! I want Dad to be with us," Davie cried.

Andie's brows drew together in a thoughtful frown. She studied her son's anxious face for several moments, then turned to Matt. "Can we speak in private for a few moments?"

Taking her cue, Brett took the baby from Sue's arms and headed for the door. "We'll take the kids outside to wait for you."

When they were gone, Andie faced Matt. "I think we need to set some boundaries."

He took a deep breath. "Such as?"

"I know we're still married, Matt, but we're separated now. We have been for a very long time."

He bit his tongue so hard it hurt. It felt like his heart sank to his knees. "I'm not asking anything from you right now, Andie. I just want to be part of your and Davie's lives."

"But you're always there, every time I turn around. I'm starting to feel claustrophobic."

He lifted one hand. "I'm sorry, sweetheart. I didn't mean to be pushy."

She shook her head. "Calling me sweetheart doesn't help. Today isn't your fault. Brett's the pushy one."

"What does Brett do for a living?"

She cleared her voice. "He's a city fireman. A captain, in fact. And very good at his job. I shouldn't be surprised the two of you get along already. You have a lot in common."

"He sounds like a good man."

"He is, but I figure Sue's giving him an ear chewing right about now." She laughed, the sound like heaven to his ears.

Matt nodded. "Don't be hard on him. I'm sure he means well. I won't come to dinner. You deserve a peaceful Sunday afternoon and I doubt you'll have that if I'm there."

A sigh of relief escaped past her lips. "Frankly I'm surprised you came to church. You never had room in your life for God. I can't help wondering if you're here to be near Davie or because you're really interested in learning about the Lord."

"Would you believe it's both?"

She peered at his face, as if trying to read the truth there. He was dead serious and hoped to convey his sincerity with his eyes.

In a change of heart, her body relaxed with resignation. "Okay, I won't fight you on coming to church. I have no right to judge you, but that doesn't resolve the problem of our marriage."

A man walked by and Matt paused, not wanting to air his personal life to strangers. Then he leaned closer to Andie and spoke low.

"I don't want a problem with you, Andie. I just want your forgiveness."

Once again, he'd laid his heart out on the chopping block, hoping she wouldn't refuse his plea.

Her blue gaze locked with his. He didn't see anger there, but a longing so intense that he figured it matched his own. Her chin quivered, a sure sign that she was about to cry. And he didn't want to make her cry ever again. He wanted to hug her.

Kiss her. Keep her safe from every sadness life threw at her.

"Look, honey, I don't mean to crowd you and Davie. I feel like a miner who's been trapped a mile underground for three months, and he's just been brought to the surface and taken his first breath of fresh air. All of this is so new to me."

She took a shuddering breath, as though his words gave her a physical blow. "I...I have to go. They're waiting for me."

"Sure, I understand." He smiled, hoping to make the situation easier on her.

He couldn't believe this had happened to them. This was the woman he'd fallen in love with, because they had so much in common and because she was so easy to talk to. Now he felt like a stranger with her.

Like an estranged husband.

She flashed him a smile of gratitude. "Thanks for understanding, Matt. But you're still invited to Davie's birthday party in a few weeks."

"I wouldn't miss it for the world. I can't believe how quickly the time has passed." He fought to keep his voice steady, so he wouldn't betray his sense of disappointment. How he wished he could climb this iron wall looming between them.

She turned and he watched her go. Every fiber of his being longed to follow her, but he had to give her some space. To slowly win her over. If he ever could.

A sense of despair engulfed him. Maybe she would never forgive him. Maybe it was too late.

Andie tucked Davie into his seat belt before driving over to Sue's house for Sunday dinner. Davie sat quietly in the backseat. Refusing to look at her. No happy chatter. No excitement about the banana cream pie Andie had made for dessert.

"What'd you talk about in Sunday school today?" she asked him.

"Forgiveness," he answered without hesitation.

Wow—usually she had to pump him for answers. But every once in a while, she realized he actually paid attention.

"Teacher said we have to forgive everyone, but God forgives who He wants to forgive," Davie said.

"That's right." She smiled at him in the rearview mirror.

"Teacher showed us a picture of a bridge and said if we can't forgive others, we break the bridge we have to cross in order to reach heaven."

Andie's breath hitched in her throat. She was starting to regret this discussion. It made her face her own biases. How could she ever forgive Matt? He seemed to be gaining the faith she'd slowly lost. And she realized that him leaving didn't excuse her from offering him forgiveness. But even if she could really forgive him, that didn't mean she wanted him to move back in with her and Davie. She didn't love him anymore. Their marriage was over.

Or was it?

Today had been more than difficult. Not in a million years did she think Matt would ever walk into a church of his own free will. Then Brett had shown him Christian compassion by inviting him to sit with the family. She'd wanted Matt to leave. To go away and leave her alone in her self-righteousness.

Matt had listened quietly to the sermons, his face almost peaceful. How could she shun her estranged husband while sitting in the Lord's house worshipping Him? She felt vile and wicked for her angry thoughts. Who had become the sinner here?

Susan pounced on her the moment they arrived at her house for dinner.

"Who does that man think he is?"

"A son of God," Brett called from the kitchen.

"You be quiet. I'm talking to my sister now." Sue bit out the words from over her shoulder before facing Andie again. "If Matt thinks he can barge back into your life and take up where he left off, he can think again."

Davie stood between them, looking at his aunt and mother with wide eyes. His little face became darker and darker, his eyes filling with angry tears.

"Sue, I don't think we should talk about this now." Andie inclined her head toward Davie.

"The boy has a right to know the truth about his father. He's no good."

"Don't talk about my daddy that way." Davie's voice trembled with hurt and anger.

"We're not, honey," Sue said. "We're talking about someone else. Someone you don't—"

"You're lying!" Davie yelled. "You hate my daddy. But he's sorry he left us. He told me so. And now he's back. Teacher said we have to forgive everyone. She said when the pottigal son returns, we should welcome him with open arms and have a big feast."

"Pottigal?" Sue's brow wrinkled in confusion. "Do you mean *prodigal?"*

Davie put his little hands on his hips, his expression furious. "That's what I said. I don't like it when you talk bad about my daddy."

Without another word, the child pushed past Andie and ran outside. The screen door slammed behind him like a shout.

Andie licked her bottom lip and tossed a glare at her sister. "Now you've done it. I asked you not to say anything bad about Matt around Davie. No matter what, Matt is Davie's father. Forever. That's not going to change, Sue."

"I'm sorry." The color drained from Sue's face.

Andie whirled about and went after her son. She doubted he'd go far, but he was young enough that she didn't want him walking or crossing a street alone. What he said was right. So far, Matt had appeared completely repentant. In fact, she felt awful for not calling to tell him they'd had a child. They both had done things wrong. They both needed forgiveness. But now, they were trying to make things easier on Davie, and Andie wouldn't hurt her son by bad-mouthing his father.

"Davie!" She pounded down the steps calling for him, but he didn't answer. Where had he gone?

She rounded the house, searching in the bushes and trees, some of his favorite hiding places.

Brett came out the back door, wearing a man's apron over his white shirt and tie. "Did you find him?"

She shook her head.

"I'll help you look." He came down the steps and skirted the yard.

"Davie! Davie, where are you?" Andie headed toward the swing set in the backyard while Brett searched the garage.

They met again in the front yard.

"No sign of him?" Andie asked.

"No, maybe he slipped back inside the house."

"I'll check with the neighbors while you check inside." Andie ran across the grass, her high heels sinking into the soft sod.

Within five minutes, she was back at Sue's house and Davie still hadn't been found. "Where would he have gone? He was so upset."

Sue sat in the rocking chair, giving a bottle to

Rose. A worried frown crinkled her brow. "I'm so sorry, Andie. I—I didn't mean to hurt his feelings."

Brett reached for his car keys. "Does he know where Matt lives?"

Andie shook her head, her skin prickling with frenzy. "No, we've never been there before. He's too little to be traipsing around town looking for his father."

Brett looked at Sue. "Honey, can you stay here in case he returns?"

"Of course. I'm so sorry." Her eyes filled with remorse.

Brett leaned down and kissed her, giving her a kind smile. "We know you are. Don't worry. Come on, Andie. You got your cell phone on?"

She nodded.

"Good. I'll take my car and you take yours. Together, we can comb more area. He couldn't have gotten far." Brett held the door open for Andie.

They left, each getting into their vehicles and driving in opposite directions. Andie wrapped her fingers tightly around the steering wheel, her heart beating madly as she peered out the windshield. She hadn't realized how loyal Davie was to his father until now. Whether she was still angry at Matt or not, she must remember that Davie loved his dad and had forgiven him.

If only she could forgive Matt as easily.

After twenty minutes, Andie dialed Brett's cell phone. He'd just spoken to Sue, but none of them had seen Davie yet. And that's when Andie called Matt. It was a last resort before she called the police.

"Hello." His deep voice helped soothe her nerves.

"Um, hi, Matt. It's Andie."

"Well, this is a pleasant surprise."

Andie almost groaned, wishing she didn't need to make this call. "I was just wondering if…if you've seen Davie in the past few minutes."

"Davie? No, I haven't seen him since I left you at church. Why?"

"He…he got upset at something his aunt said, and he ran off."

A long pause ensued. "Something she said about me?"

How did he know that? She didn't have the heart to deny it. "She hurt Davie's feelings."

Another pause. "Where have you looked for him?" His voice sounded completely calm, just like a crew leader would sound when he's figuring out a problem and the best way to resolve it.

She explained what she and Brett had done to find Davie.

"Davie's never been to my place before, so I doubt he knows where I live. Have you checked your house? He might have gone home."

"I'll check there next," she said.

"Will you call me as soon as you get there? If he's not home, I'll get in my truck and start searching, too."

"Yes." She hung up and put on her left blinker before turning the car around.

It took six minutes to get there. Tears filled her eyes when she saw her son sitting on the front steps, his elbows resting on his knees while he cupped his chin with his palms. He stared at the ground, looking so forlorn in his set of black dress slacks, sweater vest, white shirt and tie.

She got out of her car and walked to him, forcing herself not to run and scare him off again.

"Hey, hotshot. What are you doing sitting here all alone?" She sat next to him in her dress, trying to sound casual. Trying to keep the tears of relief from bursting forth.

"Nothing."

"Nothing at all?"

"Just thinking."

"You must have been real upset to have taken off like that, but don't do it again. You worried me. Next time just wait in our car, so I know you're all right."

"Okay." He still wouldn't look at her, his cheeks plumped up as he squashed his chin against his palms.

"You know Aunt Sue sometimes says things she doesn't mean, right?"

His head popped up, and his eyes narrowed angrily. "Well, she shouldn't say bad things about my dad."

"You're right, and I told her so. I don't think she'll do it again."

"What if she hurts Dad's feelings and he leaves again? I don't want him to go away. I want him to stay here forever."

Ah, now she understood. For several years, he'd been asking about his dad. Where he lived, what he did, why he didn't come home. Now that Matt was here, Davie didn't want to lose him again. Andie couldn't blame her son. A part of her wanted Matt to stay, too. She didn't want him to leave or to hurt him the way he'd hurt her. And yet, she couldn't seem to forgive him, either.

"So you ran away because you're afraid your dad might leave you?"

Davie nodded and she pulled him close against her side, holding his hand. "Your daddy would never leave you because of something Aunt Sue said. He loves you too much."

How she hoped what she said was true. How could she tell her young son that she feared the same thing? That she didn't dare open her heart and forgive Matt for his past transgressions because she feared he might leave her again? Matt had asked for her forgiveness, but he hadn't said he loved her. And she didn't want him to return out of guilt.

"Why don't you like Daddy anymore?" Davie asked.

Her breath hitched in her throat, and she had to swallow. "I like Dad just fine."

"But you don't love him."

"I—I'm not sure how I feel about him anymore. He's only been back a couple of months. We need to get to know each other again." Okay, honesty was good here.

"Then why didn't you let him come to Sunday dinner with us? Then we could get to know him better. He's all alone without us. He's probably hungry, too."

Andie swallowed a laugh. Davie's reasoning touched her heart. She'd tried to give Matt opportunity to be with Davie, but she also needed to give herself—and Sue—time to adjust to him being back in their lives.

She tried to explain to her son. "You know we were invited to dinner at Aunt Sue's house, right?"

"Yeah, we always have Sunday dinner at our place or Aunt Sue's. But I want Dad to come, too."

"I know, but it's bad manners for me to just invite your dad without permission from Aunt Sue."

"How come? Dad's part of our family. Uncle Brett said so."

She took a deep breath. "Well, Dad is part of our family, and he isn't part of our family."

"What do you mean? I heard you say you're still married to him. And he's my daddy. So that means we're his family. If we don't forgive him, who will?"

She stared, her breath leaving her in a long

whoosh. Children saw things so simply. In the Bible, the book of Matthew talked about becoming humble like a little child. Andie felt very small at that moment. According to the book of John, the Lord had given all men a new commandment to love one another. And when an adulterous woman was brought before the Lord, He asked those without sin to cast a stone at her. No one did.

Andie knew God forgave those whom He would forgive, but all men were required to forgive everyone. She had no right to withhold her forgiveness from Matt. And yet, she didn't know how to soften her heart enough to forgive him. He wasn't the only one who needed forgiveness from the Lord. Andie needed to let go of the anger and hate she'd held so closely in her heart. But how could she let it go? How could she gain enough faith to completely hand her life over to God? She longed to be able to do so, yet she didn't feel strong and courageous enough to trust the Lord that much.

"Technically you're right," she told Davie. "But your Dad's been gone so long that it's taking a bit of time for me and Aunt Sue to adjust."

"But Aunt Sue never liked Daddy. She thinks he cheated on you. When he called you, she erased his messages. I heard her say so to Uncle Brett."

Andie inhaled quickly, her stomach churning. "When did you hear her say that?"

"Last week, after she picked me up from kindergarten. What does it mean to cheat on you?"

Oh, Susan Marie Osborn! Andie couldn't believe her sister would speak her mind so freely when she knew Davie might overhear. Now it all made sense. Matt had said he'd tried to call her at home after he'd left, but Andie had never gotten any messages. Because Susan had erased them.

"Um, cheating means that your father would love another woman when he's married and promised to love only me."

Davie's mouth rounded. "Daddy wouldn't cheat on you, Mom. He loves us. I know he does."

"Don't you worry. I'll take care of it, okay?" If she and Matt still loved each other, maybe she could forgive him and they could be a real family again.

Wishful thinking. They were a long way away from that happening.

A truck pulled up in front of the house, and Matt stepped out with the aid of his cane. "Looks like you found him."

"Daddy!" Davie ran to his father and threw his arms around Matt's legs.

Matt tottered, almost losing his balance. "Hey, easy there, hotshot. What's going on?"

Together they walked to the porch, and he met Andie's gaze as she stood to meet them. Matt bent over and picked Davie up in his free arm, using his cane to shuffle over to the porch swing. As he walked, he listened to Davie pour his big, aching heart out about what had happened. Andie hated for Matt to know how Sue had hurt Davie's feelings, but there was no help for it. If Andie tried to hush Davie, the boy might think she agreed with her sister. And she did, to a certain point. She didn't want to get back together with Matt, but she didn't want Sue to bad-mouth her husband, either. After all, Matt had a lot of good qualities. He wasn't an ogre. He was a good man who had gotten a few priorities out of whack.

"You won't leave again, will you, Dad?" Davie sniffed and wiped his nose on his shirtsleeve.

Matt hugged the boy close and kissed his hair. "No, I'll never leave you again. Not ever."

Davie peered at his mom, a triumphant look in his eyes. "See, Mom. I told ya."

She smiled, wanting so much to believe what Matt said. "Yes, you did tell me that."

Matt had called her. He'd left her messages she'd never received. Andie had misjudged him. She couldn't believe it. Part of her wanted to berate Sue for hiding this information for so long. Another part of her wanted to just let it all go. None of it mattered anymore.

Brett pulled into the driveway and jumped out, looking relieved. He jerked his apron off before sauntering up the front walkway. "Well, it looks like we've got almost everyone here. Maybe we should have Sunday dinner at your house today."

"Hi, Uncle Brett. What are you doing here?" Davie asked.

"Looking for you, champ. Aunt Sue feels real bad for hurting your feelings. We were all mighty worried when you ran off like that."

"Sorry." The boy sat up straight and slid off his dad's lap.

"He won't do it again, will you, son?" Matt smiled, a look of pure love filling his eyes.

Andie looked away. Whether she liked it or not, her two boys loved each other. Very much. She'd have to make room for Matt in her life, even if they didn't get back together again.

Brett stood before them, the apron crumpled in his fist. "Tell you what. Why don't we all go back to my house and enjoy our Sunday dinner? We've had enough drama for one day."

Matt frowned and so did Davie.

"I'm not sure that's such a good idea. I don't think I'm welcome there," Matt said.

"Of course you are. I just talked to Sue on the cell, and she said I wasn't to come home without you. So come on. She feels bad enough. Let's do what families should do and forgive one another, okay?"

Andie froze. Brett had always been so easygoing. A peacemaker who lived to make Sue happy. But his sense of justice had forced him to challenge Sue on this issue. He spoke of forgiving one another. That's what families did, right? And that's what it came down to for Andie. Forgiveness.

If she couldn't forgive Matt, where did that leave her with the Lord?

Davie looked at Matt. "I'll go back if you will."

A hysterical laugh bubbled up in Andie's throat. She could definitely force Davie to go to Sue's house or go to his room. But she didn't want to lose her son's love. And right now, she realized he was so relieved to have his father back in his life that he might defy her if she refused. She wanted to make her son happy, but that wasn't a reason to invite Matt back into their marriage. She had to be certain they loved each other and wouldn't hurt each other again.

And that brought Andie's brain to a standstill. How could they go through the many years ahead without ever being thoughtless? Without saying some insensitive remark or doing something that hurt the other person's feelings? They couldn't. Marriage was a process. It wasn't perfect, and it took daily, hard work to maintain. No guarantees. That's how families worked. But if they loved each other—really loved each other—they could continue to forgive each other over and over again. They could be happy. Right?

"That's a good idea, son. It's the Sabbath and we should be happy today." Andie reached out and took Davie's hand.

Davie followed her to the car, as if everything was settled. But Matt hung back, an expression of doubt creasing his eyes.

"Come on. You're with me." Brett clapped Matt on the shoulder.

Matt followed, but he didn't look happy about it. They all piled into Brett's car, and no one spoke during the ride back to Sue's house. Inside, Sue avoided Matt and said very little, but she did quietly apologize to Davie in the kitchen.

The boy kissed Sue on the cheek and ran off to play with little Rose. Watching him go, Andie couldn't help but think how much Davie was like his father. Matt had never been one to hold a grudge, either. In the early years of their marriage, she'd envied him this quality. Now she wasn't so sure.

Dinner was a subdued affair. Brett did most of the talking.

"How long have you been fighting fire?" Brett asked.

"More than ten years." Matt took a bite of tender roast beef, looking at his plate. He seemed reticent to talk about his fire days.

"Me, too. But I suppose our training is a bit different, since I mostly fight building fires. There've been a few times when the Forest Service called on the city for help fighting a big wildfire."

"We may call on you again sometime. I'm the FCO and trying to coordinate our efforts in case we ever need city help."

Brett nodded. "Give me a call next week and we can set up a meeting to talk. I'd be glad to help any way we can. Maybe we can have lunch."

"It's a deal." Matt smiled.

The two men seemed to get along well, monopolizing the discussion as they talked about work and baseball. Andie noticed Sue occupied herself with feeding the baby and serving everyone else.

When dinner ended, Andie helped clean up the kitchen while the men and Davie disappeared into the family room to watch baseball on TV.

Andie handed the platter of meat to her sister while they cleared the table. "You seem awful quiet tonight, sis."

Sue tucked a curl of hair behind her ear. "I don't have a lot to say."

"Not even about Matt's phone calls you erased?"

The color drained from Sue's face, her eyes filled with fear. She'd been caught. "Davie told you about that?"

Andie nodded. "Why did you do it, Sue? Matt called me. He cared. If I'd known, we might have gotten back together years ago. We could have talked things through."

"I'm sorry, Andie. I—I could only see the bad in him. I thought you were better off without him."

"And Davie? You thought he was better off without his father?"

"Yes—no—I don't know. By then, it was too late." Sue groaned and covered her face with her hands.

Andie hugged her sister. "It's in the past. Let's forget about it now. On one condition."

Sue looked at her sister, her eyes filled with tears of remorse. "And what's that?"

"That you never come between my husband and me again. Ever."

"Agreed. I'll never erase a message, throw away a note or prevent Matt from speaking with you again. I'm so sorry, Andie. For everything."

"Then all is forgiven."

Sue drew back, her eyes filled with sadness. "You can forgive me so easily?"

"Of course. You're my sister. The only one I have."

"But I drove Davie away. What I said hurt his feelings, and he could have been seriously injured when he walked home alone. Thank goodness we live in a small town and he got there safely."

"Don't worry about it anymore. We're all safe and sound."

"Are we, Andie? Are we really?"

"Of course."

Sue jutted her chin toward the family room. "And what about Matt? I hate what he did to you. I was there when he left you. And when Davie was born. I remember how you cried. How he broke your heart. I don't want to see him hurt you again. You can forgive me, but why can't I forgive him?"

Andie bit her bottom lip. She felt the same way, but she didn't want to cry about this today. Or ever again. She wanted to put it behind her. Could forgiveness be that simple? Could she just let it go?

"I know, Sue. I don't think Matt's going away this time, even if he leaves town. He'll always be Davie's daddy. I just want to find a way to make this easier on all of us."

"I know. But what about you? How are you going to deal with this situation? You're still young, Andie. You deserve to be with someone who loves you."

Andie smiled, trying to be strong. Trying to reach for the faith she'd slowly lost over years of lethargy toward God. "I'm going to start rebuilding my trust in the Lord. And from there, I'll deal with it one day at a time."

Chapter Nine

Matt grit his teeth as he lay on his back and pressed his knee against the exercise mat in his physical therapist's office. In his head, he counted to twenty, then released a breath of air as he relaxed his leg.

"Good, but keep your heel pressed down. We need to strengthen your thigh." Shane, his therapist, used his strong hands to knead the tight muscles of Matt's calf.

Matt did as told, determined to toughen his bad leg so he could walk without a cane. For weeks he'd been walking on his treadmill, gradually increasing the pace until he was jogging three miles every day. It wasn't easy, but he could do it as long as he held tight to the handrails. Whenever he thought of letting go, he reminded himself that he was holding on to his faith in God, and nothing was impossible with the Lord on his side.

Now as he repeated the exercise, his thigh

muscle screamed in agony. Matt clenched his hands, counting to twenty-five, determined to push himself. He had to get himself in condition to deal with the fire-fighting training school he had planned in early May.

It seemed to take a century to finish each set, but Matt did it. He wanted to cry like a baby, but he refused to quit. He might have to live with chronic pain the rest of his life, but he couldn't give in to it. Not unless he wanted to commit suicide to find relief. He'd thought of that option many times during the first couple of months following the wildfire. But when he imagined never seeing Andie again, the idea of killing himself had flown out the window. And now there was Davie to think about.

Matt wanted to live. Wanted to be whole again. He would pass the arduous level of his physical testing next month. He would!

Though he hadn't found a way to forgive himself for what happened during the wildfire, and he hadn't won Andie's forgiveness, he had found the courage to keep trying. Whenever he thought of giving up, a curious peace settled over him, giving him strength to fight off the despair. To keep going.

Shane released the pressure and gently massaged Matt's thigh. "You're getting stronger, Matt. I can see a big difference this week. Rest a moment. You feel like doing another set?"

"Sure." No, he didn't really, but Matt breathed in deeply, easing himself through the tight muscles.

Dressed in exercise shorts, he turned his head away so he wouldn't have to look at the ugly scars marring his flesh. At one time, he'd been in superb physical condition with strong, muscular legs. When not working on a fire, he'd had a fitness regime that included push-ups, sit-ups and chin-ups. He'd run ten miles on his days off, pushing himself further and harder than any of his crew members. Now every movement seemed a major undertaking.

"Yep, you're definitely getting stronger, Matt. I can tell you've been doing your exercises at home."

"I never miss a day." Not when it meant he might walk like a normal man again.

"How many repetitions are you up to with each set?"

"Twenty before I rest."

"How many sets?"

"Thirty sets three times a day."

Shane stared at Matt, then gave a low whistle. "No wonder you're stronger. But how's the pain?"

"Like a mother bear."

"Not getting any better?"

Matt wished. "Not yet. Maybe it's just my toleration for pain that has increased."

Shane's strong fingers continued to knead the taut muscles in Matt's leg. "Hang in there, Matt. I hate to say this to one of my patients, but you may be pushing yourself too hard. I'm hoping your muscles reach a point where they no longer hurt. They were badly damaged and need time to repair."

They started another set of exercises with Matt pressing against Shane's strong hands. Matt breathed deep and slow, clenching his jaw. Shane kept up a steady stream of conversation, and Matt realized it was Shane's way of distracting him from the pain.

"How's your family doing?" Shane leaned his weight forward against Matt's lifted leg.

"Good." Matt thought about Davie's birthday party coming up soon. He couldn't wait.

"You still having nightmares?"

"Yeah." For some reason, Matt had confided in Shane the first time he met him after Shane suggested Matt might want to depend upon a higher power than himself to get through his rehabilitation. The physical therapist had an easy, nonjudgmental way about him that made Matt feel safe. Before Matt even realized what he was doing, he'd revealed that he was having nightmares about the wildfire.

"Did you tell your doctor about them?"

"I haven't had time to see a shrink yet."

Shane waved his hand, and Matt rolled over onto his stomach. They both had this routine down flat. Matt knew the exercises by heart. "Talking to a medical professional is just as important to your psychological health as these exercises are to your physical health."

"I don't need some shrink to analyze my mind. I know how I feel. I don't need someone telling me how I should feel." Matt bent his knee, pressing the heel of his left foot toward the back of his thigh.

Shane waited to see if Matt could lift the flat of his foot up toward the ceiling without assistance. Matt could do it, but he couldn't hold it for long before his hamstring cramped like a knotted rope.

"I think a psychologist would help you deal with your mental pain, Matt. Sometimes we think we have all the answers when we don't. A trained professional can help you discover how to feel better."

"I don't have time," Matt grumbled, knowing Shane was right. Matt had always had the answers before. He wasn't used to asking for help from strangers and didn't want to start now.

Shane assisted Matt, lifting and pressing gently but firmly. "You need to make time, Matt. I've read your report, and what happened on the wildfire wasn't your fault. It's important that you forgive yourself. It'll help with your rehabilitation."

Matt didn't respond. How could he forgive himself when every fiber of his being disagreed? When a good man had died?

"How did church go last week?" Shane asked.

Matt had also confided to Shane that he planned to attend church. "Fine, after my wife and sister-in-law got over the shock of seeing me in a church."

Shane chuckled. "Yeah, I have one of those sisters-in-law myself. And a mother-in-law, too. Did attending church help you with the nightmares?"

Not a lot. Though Matt had found solace in reaching out to God, he hadn't yet resolved his survivor's guilt. Why had he lived when Jim had died? The other man had a family depending on him. His wife and kids needed him. And yet, Matt had been the one to survive. Why?

Though Matt hadn't yet found the answer, he believed it had something to do with his return to Andie and discovering he had a son. Maybe God had saved him so that Matt could become a father to Davie. Could it be that simple?

"And what about your wife?"

Shane's words echoed in Matt's hollow heart. He'd been thinking the same thing. Davie had welcomed Matt with open arms, but Andie remained aloof. Matt wondered if he'd ever break through her defenses and mend her broken heart. Since last week, he'd repeatedly asked God for help, but maybe it was too late. Matt couldn't pray away Andie's free agency. God allowed all men and women, both good and bad, to choose for themselves how they would act. Sometimes their actions injured other people. Andie had the right to decide for herself, but perhaps the Lord could soften her heart.

"I'm not sure if Andie will ever forgive me, but

at least she's speaking to me. And she lets me visit my son almost any time I want."

"That's good. Don't give up on her. I can help rehabilitate your injured body, but the Lord can help mend Andie's angry heart. And a trained psychologist can help rehabilitate your injured mind."

Matt gave a dry laugh. "You never give up, do you?"

Shane flashed a grin. "Not on my favorite patients. I figure we're also friends."

"We are. You don't by chance know any exercises I can do to gain Andie's forgiveness, do you?"

"Yeah, as a matter of fact, I do."

"Oh? What's the secret?"

"Send lots of knee mail."

"Knee mail?"

Shane smiled. "Yeah, prayer. You know? Get down on your knees and pray. It'll be good exercise for your soul as well as your leg muscles. Then trust in your higher power to do the rest. Give it time. You just need the courage to work through everything."

Matt snorted. "What about Andie's will?"

"If you're willing to accept the will of your higher power, your heart and soul will be equipped to accept Andie's will also."

Shane's words sank deep into Matt's heart. Could it be true? Could he really accept God's will if it meant Andie continued to harden her heart against him?

Matt figured he had little choice in what Andie decided to do. But he could choose to be happy even if Andie refused to forgive him. And that's when Matt realized that his love for Andie wasn't conditional upon her love for him. He loved her no matter what, because his love was all he had control over. He could decide, irrespective of what other people in his life chose to do. He had his freedom to choose, no matter what hardships or pain he faced. No matter what other people chose to do.

He could still choose to be happy and to love his family.

Matt sat up on the exercise mat and Shane helped him stand. Matt put his weight on his bad leg, testing its strength. After his heavy workout, his legs felt surprisingly relaxed and pain-free today. Maybe the therapy was helping after all. "I sure hope you're right, Shane."

"I know I am."

His friend's confidence inspired Matt. By the time he left the physical therapist's office, he felt renewed and hopeful. As he walked out to the parking lot, his leg didn't cramp, and he took every fourth step without leaning on his cane. Tonight he'd do his exercises at home, in hopes that his muscles wouldn't tighten up through the night. Tomorrow he planned to start hiking. He'd wear a vest, gradually adding weight over the next few weeks until he could carry forty-five pounds for three miles and cover the distance within forty-five minutes. That's what it would take for him to pass the arduous level of his fitness requirement.

As he climbed into his truck, he felt surprisingly free for the first time in months. The weight of surviving the wildfire didn't seem as gloomy as before. He'd been given an awesome gift. The gift of life. A chance to change. To become a better man.

A man of God.

In spite of all his faults, Matt was determined not to let the Lord down again.

Andie glanced at the brass clock hanging on her office wall and gasped. Eleven-fifteen. How had the time gotten away from her so fast?

She clicked the save button on her computer screen and closed the mineral study she'd been working on for the Forest Supervisor. After tidying some reports on her desk, she hurried to the lady's room to freshen up. Matt would be here by eleven-thirty, and she didn't want to be late.

In the restroom, she couldn't help checking her appearance in the mirror. She brushed the long bangs back from her face and rubbed away a smudge of mascara. Her eyes still looked puffy with fatigue, but that couldn't be helped now.

Hurrying back to her office, she stopped by Clarice's desk to give her some last-minute instructions on where she'd be for the rest of the afternoon.

"I'm riding out to visit Hank Cleary at Cove Ranch. Matt Cutter will be with me. You can reach me on my cell phone if something important comes up."

Clarice lifted a perfectly manicured hand and pointed toward Andie's office. "He's waiting for you now."

Andie tilted her head. "Hank Cleary?"

"No, Matt Cutter. He's in your office. He just arrived a few minutes ago."

Andie's heart beat faster. Matt was early. "Okay, I'll see you tomorrow morning."

As she headed to her office, Andie forced herself not to rush. For some reason, knowing Matt was waiting for her made her want to hurry, but she didn't want to appear anxious to see him. Which she wasn't.

Okay, maybe a little. But only because she was worried about him. Which irritated her. She didn't want to worry about her husband. Worrying led to caring, which led to love, and she couldn't allow herself to care for Matt ever again.

"Hi, Andie." He smiled that lopsided smile of his when she entered the room. A smile that deepened the dimple in his left cheek and lit up his blue eyes.

In spite of what she'd just told herself, she couldn't deny his presence made her feel happier. He sat in a chair before her desk, wearing his Forest Service uniform and grasping the hilt of his cane.

She looked away. "Hi, Matt. Ready to go?"

She shut down her computer, knowing she probably wouldn't return before closing. The drive to and from Cove Ranch would take more than two hours, plus discussion and contract time.

Matt stood and opened the door for her. It might be her imagination, but he didn't seem to limp quite as much.

"How's your leg feeling today?" she asked as they walked outside to the parking lot.

"Better. I just left physical therapy, which loosens the muscles up."

"So therapy is helping?"

He shrugged one shoulder. "Quite a bit. I'm hopeful."

In the parking lot, she stared at her car with indecision. "You want to take mine or yours?"

"Mine." He didn't break stride as he walked toward the farthest corner of the lot. Parked beneath an ornamental cherry tree in full bloom was his blue truck.

"You sure you can drive that far with your bad leg?"

"Yep." He kept walking, and she recognized the stubborn set of his shoulders.

"You sure parked a long way from the door." She hustled to keep up with his brisk stride, pleased to see him moving more freely.

"Doctor's orders. I do it on purpose to exercise my leg."

Smart. "It seems to be working."

"Yes, but after therapy, the leg usually stiffens on me in the night. Tomorrow morning, it'll probably be stiffer than ever. So I might as well enjoy today." He flashed her a smile and dug the keys out of his pants pocket.

The truck beeped as he used the remote to unlock the doors. He swung the door to the passenger seat open for her and she climbed in.

She should ask him about the wildfire now while he seemed willing to talk. But how did she do that without appearing too interested?

He walked around the truck and got inside, then buckled his seat belt before starting the engine. She held on to the armrest as he pulled onto Main Street and headed outside of town.

He glanced at her. "You look tired today. Everything okay at home?"

It seemed odd that he knew so much about her personal life. And even odder that he could tell she hadn't slept well the night before.

She brushed a hand across her green shirt, feeling self-conscious. For some reason, she didn't like looking tired in front of this man. She wanted him to find her young and attractive. Now, that was a crazy notion after all these years. "Davie kept me up most of the night. He has an upset stomach and didn't go to school today."

Matt raised one dark eyebrow. "Anything serious?"

"I don't think so. Sue called me about thirty minutes ago and said he's not throwing up anymore. He's sucking on a homemade ice pop and watching cartoons."

"Good. I'd hate for him to be sick for his birthday."

"You still planning to come to the party?"

He flashed a smile. "I wouldn't miss it! What can I bring?"

"Nothing. Just yourself."

"Is there anything in particular Davie's been wanting for a present?"

"Only everything in sight."

He laughed, a deep bass sound that reminded her of low thunder just before a rainstorm on the mountain. "He's a normal kid, then."

"He doesn't need everything. I don't want to spoil him, so please don't go overboard on gifts."

"I agree." He paused, glancing in his rearview mirror. "How many big tractors does Hank Cleary have?"

She blinked, reminding herself that they were driving out to Cove Ranch to take a look at Mr. Cleary's large cats, not to discuss her personal life. "Two, both with disc plows on them. From what my range specialist told me, Hank's always been a big help during wildfires. He and his son are experienced and know how to build fire line quickly."

"And you've already spoken to him, to see if he's willing to let us contract his equipment again this year?"

"Of course, by phone. He's a nice man and easy to work with."

She fidgeted, wondering how to broach the subject that was really on her mind. She decided to just ask. "Matt, I don't mean to be nosy, but have you ever told anyone what happened on the wildfire when you were injured?"

He tensed and hardened his jaw, his eyes narrowed and alert. "I've told the Lord."

"And that's all?"

"That's all I need."

"But maybe a professional could also help you."

His gaze bit into hers. "Help me with what? Who have you been talking to, Andie?"

"I, um…" She didn't want to tell him that she'd called Ken. Matt might think she was prying into his life. Or that she cared about him. "I heard that one of your men died on that fire and figured you might need someone to talk to about it. I know how I'd feel if I lost a crewman."

"No, you can't prepare for that, Andie. No one really knows how they'd feel until it happens to them."

"Well, I know I'd feel rotten inside. Maybe even guilty because I'd survived when one of my men had died."

His expression darkened, his profile hard as granite. That alone told her she'd hit the nail on the head. "It's not your fault, Matt. It happened, that's all. You shouldn't blame yourself."

"You don't understand." He shook his head, gazing out the windshield, refusing to meet her eyes.

"Then tell me. I'm trying to understand, Matt."

"No you're not, Andie. You don't want to understand anything about me. Not anymore. You wish I'd never darkened your doorstep and come back into your life."

His voice had lowered to an angry growl. They'd been parted for a long time, but she still knew him well enough to detect the anguish he tried to hide. If she'd been a vindictive person, she should be glad he was hurting. Instead, she felt sorrow for his pain and longed to help him recover.

"Yes, I am trying to understand. Really I am. I—I've been hurting just like you," she said. "When you returned, I wasn't prepared, that's all. I certainly don't wish you harm. And no matter what happens between us, Davie needs his father. I think you should consider getting some professional help, just to make sure you're feeling happy and content inside."

Her concession seemed to soften him some small bit. His grip on the steering wheel relaxed slightly, his knuckles no longer white.

"I'm sorry, Andie. I didn't mean to bite at you. I'm dealing with what happened in my own way. I just wish everyone would stop telling me what I need."

"Okay, okay," she conceded. "Then you tell me. What do you need, Matt?"

"My family," he responded without hesitation.

Great! She'd blundered into this discussion without thinking it through. She had no one to blame but herself. He'd always been brutally honest. Why should she be surprised now?

"You can visit Davie anytime you want."

"And what about you?" He looked at her, his eyes filled with contrition and hope.

"I…I don't know what you're getting at. We're married in name only, Matt."

"I think I've already made it clear that I'd like to change that. I'd like to be a real family again, living under one roof." She opened her mouth to speak, but he lifted a hand to cut her off. "Don't say anything right now, Andie. I know we both need more time to get to know one another again and for me to prove I won't run out on you again. I just want you to know that I'm in this for keeps this time." He emphasized his words.

Now it was her turn to face forward and ignore his searching look. He was asking her for something she didn't think she could give. Certainly not without love, which he hadn't mentioned.

"What other fire equipment will you need this summer?" he asked.

The quick change of topic wasn't lost on Andie. He'd had his say and now wanted to move on, as if he feared she might turn him down flat and never broach the subject again.

Because she didn't want to talk about their relationship, she played along. She rattled off a verbal list. Various equipment, heavy machinery, catering of meals and portable toilets her fire crews would need in case of a wildfire.

By the time they arrived at Cove Ranch, she felt like a caged tiger ready to jump out of the closed confines of Matt's truck. They met with Mr. Cleary, signed the contracts to use his large cats during fire season and returned to town without any more discussion about their family, or lack thereof.

Instead, Matt and Andie reminisced about funny stories during their experiences fighting wildfire. "Remember that time Ken set his tent on fire?"

Andie couldn't help laughing. "As I recall, a skunk had gotten inside. Ken insisted on using those old-fashioned flame lanterns. When he went inside the tent, the skunk surprised him and he dropped the lantern."

Matt chuckled, deep and low in his chest. "If not for your quick thinking, the whole forest could have burned down. Good thing you grabbed that bucket of water and doused the flames when you did. I don't know what surprised Ken more—the skunk, or being drenched with a bucket of icy water."

Andie pressed a hand over her eyes and shook

her head. She laughed, remembering the good times they'd shared. They'd been so happy. So in love.

And just as quickly, her laughter turned to tears. She turned away so Matt wouldn't see. So he wouldn't know how much she mourned their lost years together. If only she could put aside the hurt and regain that love. But she just didn't know how.

Chapter Ten

On Saturday morning, Matt arrived early at Taylor Park, across the street from the elementary school. April twenty-second. Davie's birthday. Matt would never forget this date as long as he lived.

He felt good today. He'd hiked three miles in forty-five minutes wearing a pack with thirty pounds of weight. He'd fallen once, wrenching his leg, but hopped back up and kept going. The leg had held, hurting him less, and he was optimistic. If everything progressed as planned, he figured he'd be able to pass his fire-training conditioning physical in three weeks.

As he pulled his truck into the parking lot, he could make out Andie standing on a low ladder, tying balloons to the pavilion near the playground. A large, curved sign hung over her head that read Happy Birthday Davie. Nearby, Davie pushed little Rose around in her stroller. The baby waved her chubby arms and smiled. Davie clapped his hands, then threw back his head and laughed when the baby copied him.

A flood of warmth enveloped Matt's chest. He could think of no place on earth he'd rather be than here with his family. He watched Rose with curiosity, wishing he'd been here the day Davie was born. Wishing he and Andie could have more children together.

It took a minute for Matt to gather several packages in his arms. No cane today. Since he'd exercised hard that morning, he moved slowly, resting his legs, fearing his thigh might start cramping up on him and ruin his day.

He gazed at the assortment of other gifts sitting on the backseat of his truck and planned to make several trips to retrieve them all. Andie wouldn't approve of spoiling Davie, but Matt couldn't seem to help himself. He could just imagine what she'd say when she discovered the gift he'd set up in Davie's bedroom while they were here at the park. Matt justified the presents by telling himself he'd missed too many birthdays and Christmases with his wife and son.

As he approached the picnic area, he saw Brett carrying a large cardboard box toward the pavilion.

"Where do you want the games set up?" Brett called to Andie.

A roll of red crepe paper dangled from Andie's

hand as she pointed toward the grass. "We'll want the water balloons and relay races over there, away from the food."

Knowing his sister-in-law would undoubtedly be here, Matt scanned the area for Susan. She wasn't here. Yet. Matt locked down his temper with an iron will, determined not to be baited or offended by Sue. His love for Andie and Davie was more important than his ego. He refused to bite back if Sue said something insulting to him.

Brett set the box down on a picnic table and looked up. "Hey, Matt! Glad you're here. You can give me a hand."

Matt blinked, still surprised by Brett's open friendliness. At least he had two allies—Brett and Davie—which gave him the confidence to jump in and help out.

"Dad! Are those for me?" Davie let go of Rose's stroller and ran over to his father, eyeing the gifts Matt carried.

"Nope, they're for the birthday boy," Matt teased.

"But I'm the birthday boy." Davie hopped up and down with excitement.

Matt set the gifts on the table, pretending to play dumb. "You are? But I thought it was some other little boy's birthday today."

Davie giggled and picked up one of the presents, giving it a good shake. "No, you didn't. You know it's my birthday. What did you get me?"

Matt ruffled the boy's hair. "It's a surprise, hot-shot. Don't shake them too hard. You might break something."

Andie stepped down from the ladder and rested a hand on her hip. She looked ravishing yet casual in blue jeans and sneakers, her hair hanging in loose curls around her shoulders.

"Where's your cane?"

He shrugged, delighted that she'd noticed. "I don't think I need it today."

Longing to share his good news with her, he told her about his successful hike earlier.

"You're sure you're not pushing too hard? You don't need to pass the arduous level of the fitness test to serve as the Operations Section Chief on a NIIMS." NIIMS stood for National Interagency Incident Management System, for wildland fire-fighting.

"I know, but I do need to pass the moderate physical, which still requires a two-mile hike wearing a twenty-five-pound pack within thirty minutes. So I figured I'd work toward the arduous level."

She snorted. "I'm not surprised. Mediocre never was your style." She eyed the presents he'd brought with him. "How many gifts did you get him?" A frown of disapproval curved her pretty mouth, but her eyes glowed with happiness, and Matt knew she wasn't really upset.

"Just a few." Matt decided to leave the other gifts in his truck for the time being. Maybe he could sneak them into the pile later on, when Andie was busy with Davie and his guests.

Matt looked up at the sky where a few gray clouds floated above. "Looks like we're gonna have good weather for the party."

Andie glanced skyward and wrapped her arms around her. "Thank goodness. I feared I might have to think up some games to play inside my house, which wouldn't give us much room to move. It's still a bit chilly outside."

Matt doffed his jacket and slipped it over her slender shoulders. "No worries. By the time the guests arrive, the sun will warm things up."

She clutched the folds of his jacket and looked away, her face turning a pretty shade of pink. She blinked, looking shy. Like a young girl flirting with a boy. But she hadn't rejected his offering, and Matt almost shouted with joy.

"Did Sue go to pick up the cake?" Brett walked over to them.

"Yeah, she should be back any minute." Andie slid her arms into the sleeves of Matt's oversize jacket, then struggled with the roll of crepe paper.

Matt loved seeing her wearing his clothes. It reminded him of a happier time when she'd worn his long T-shirts around the house in the morning or slipped his large slippers on her bare feet so she could go outside to move the sprinkler on the grass.

As she endeavored to twist a strand of yellow with red crepe paper to create a streamer around the pavilion, Matt reached for one end. "Let me help."

He held on tight while she twisted the two colors together. Then he supported the ladder while she climbed up and stapled the ends to the wooden pavilion. When she stepped down, she lost her footing and he clasped her arm to prevent her from falling. The extra weight wrenched his bad leg, but it didn't hurt as much as usual. Maybe the exercises were finally strengthening the muscles. Maybe he could beat this physical weakness after all.

"Sorry," she murmured as she stepped away.

Her hair brushed against his face, soft and fragrant, setting off every nerve in his body. He smiled, trying to put her at ease. "No problem."

"Hey, Matt. Can you barbecue?" Brett asked.

Matt grinned. "With the best of them."

"Good. While I fill the balloons with water, you're in charge of the briquettes. We're serving hamburgers and hotdogs to the kids and their parents." Brett indicated a bag of briquettes and lighter fluid sitting on the ground.

"Got it." Matt walked over to the grill, grateful to be given an assignment he could negotiate well.

"This will be a good opportunity for you to meet all of Andie's friends. It should be fun," Brett said.

"How many guests are we having?"

"About ten kids and their parents."

Matt didn't respond. He used to enjoy gatherings like this, but since the wildfire, he'd started shying away from large crowds. He reminded himself that he wasn't limping as noticeably anymore. He didn't have to explain the cane to anyone. Because he desperately wanted to be included in every facet of his wife and son's lives, he'd forced himself to push his own self-doubts aside. His physical therapist had told him a good attitude was everything, and Matt was determined to choose to be happy.

By the time Sue arrived with the birthday cake, Matt had lit the coals and scoured off the grill. As she passed by carrying a large, flat box, he tensed, hoping she'd ignore him. He wanted no harsh words to spoil Davie's party.

"You want to see?"

Matt almost choked when she stepped near and lifted the lid for him to peek inside. The large sheet cake had been decorated like a baseball field with diamonds, gloves, bats and balls. Six blue candles were centered by home plate. "That's great. Davie will love it."

"I want to see." Davie came running.

"Nope, sorry. Not until it's time to blow out your candles." Sue smiled as she snapped the lid back onto the box and carried it to the table.

"Ah!" The boy groaned and followed her.

"Don't worry, sweetheart. You'll get to open everything. We just want to have a fun surprise for you." Andie spread several blue-and-red plastic tablecloths across the tables, weighing them down with packages of buns and bottles of condiments.

Davie smiled and gazed at the growing pile of gifts with anticipation.

"Matt, can you help me lift a cooler from my car?" Sue called to him and he turned in surprise.

Sue was speaking to him. Why? She hated him. Why didn't she ask Brett for help instead?

"Sure." He followed her to the parking lot, a little skeptical and anxious. Out of his peripheral vision, Matt saw Andie watching them with a nervous frown.

"I remember you always preferred water to soda pop, so I got plenty of bottles of water, and juice boxes, too. I hope we planned enough food. You never know how many people will show up at these things." Sue kept up a steady stream of small talk as she popped the trunk of her car open.

Bracing his knees against the bumper, Matt lifted the weight of the cooler up over the edge of the trunk. Then they each took hold of a handle on the sides of the cooler.

As Matt carried his end, he moved slowly, almost disbelieving when his leg didn't hurt one bit. He remembered a time not so long ago when he could have carried the cooler by himself. Now he felt euphoric, thinking he might regain full use of his limbs.

Patience, man. Patience.

"Thanks." Sue gave him a half smile as they set the cooler on the cement slab beside the tables.

"You're welcome." Matt returned to his grill, confused and worried. Was Sue trying to make up for bad-mouthing him to Davie? Or did she have other motives?

Guests started arriving, little wriggling boys and girls accompanied by their parents. Brett introduced Matt as Davie's father to each and every one. Andie didn't say a word, and Brett didn't apologize for being so blunt. But Andie seemed a bit quieter than usual. Matt knew her moods well enough to know she was perturbed. The tight mouth and reluctance in her blue eyes were a dead giveaway. She'd always been a private person. Maybe she didn't like her friends knowing Davie's father was here. It roused too many questions about their marriage.

"Okay, kids. Who wants to play some games?" Brett's buoyant voice filled the air, and the kids cheered as they raced after him to the grass.

Matt followed, listening as Brett explained the rules of the bucket-and-sponge relay race. The dads joined them while the moms congregated with their smaller children over at the pavilion, helping Andie and Sue set out potato chips and fruit salad.

Shrill laughter rang throughout the park as they began the races. In between checking on the briquettes, Matt helped disperse candy and prizes to the kids. As he watched his son wolf down a piece of taffy, he chuckled. "I doubt these kids will eat much lunch after this."

Brett flashed a wide grin. "It's okay this time. It's a special occasion."

It certainly was. The day of his son's birth. How he wished he had been with his wife six years earlier.

Before long, the men were threatening their wives with water balloons heavy with water. Children chased each other around with dripping sponges. Squeals filled the air. Matt joined in, playing with the children, protecting the girls from the boys, and generally having a great time. When a fat, green water balloon hit him square in the chest, he gasped and looked up.

Andie stood in front of him, her eyes large and round, a hand clasped across her mouth in shock. She shook her head with disbelief. "I'm sorry, I didn't mean to do that. I—I was aiming at Brett."

Brett stepped back and lifted his hands as if to give himself up. "Don't blame this on me."

Matt narrowed his eyes at his wife, a vindictive smile widening his mouth. "Yeah, sure. You were aiming at Brett. Uh-huh, I believe that."

He reached behind his back and took out the secret weapon he'd stowed beneath his shirt—a squirt gun. Knowing they were going to have water balloons, he'd come prepared.

Andie's eyes widened when she saw the water

gun. As he stalked toward her, she backed away, her hands in the air. "Now, Matt. Be nice."

"Be nice? You're telling me to be nice after what you just did?" He wiped a hand across his soaking-wet shirt.

She turned and ran. He took off after her, clasping an arm around her slim waist. He pressed the trigger, spraying a stream of water at her cheek. He could have drenched her, but decided to play nice.

She squealed with laughter and ran to pick up another water balloon. They sparred for several minutes, until he pulled her close and hugged her tight. Her happy laughter filled his senses to over-flowing. It was as if no one existed in the world but him and her.

When he let her go, she returned to the pavilion, but he soon found himself under assault again by her and some of the kids. He fled, but not before he was soaked, his jeans dragging with water. He bided his time. If nothing else, his lame leg had taught him patience.

Andie moved over to the tables where the women sat together in a group, hoping their husbands left them alone. Matt chuckled to himself and waited. Keeping a water balloon close by, he went to check the white briquettes. He tossed ham-burger patties and hot dogs on the grill, flipping them like a pro. Brett offered him a bottle of water, and several men stood around drinking sodas and chatting with him.

"So you're in the Forest Service?" Carl Baxter asked.

"Yeah, in the Supervisor's office."

"When did you and Andie get divorced?"

Wow! Talk about blunt. Matt used the pretense of turning hot dogs as an excuse to look away. "We didn't."

Carl frowned. "So you're still married?"

Matt didn't respond. Somehow he knew Andie wouldn't approve of this line of questions.

Brett interceded by lifting the platter piled high with meat. "I think we've got enough food here to get started. Let's eat."

Thank you, Brett! Matt met the other man's gaze and nodded his thanks. Brett smiled in understanding.

"Matt, since you're the head of your family, would you like to offer a blessing on the food?" Brett asked.

Matt almost fell over flat. He felt the blood drain from his face, and a trembling that had nothing to do with being wet and cold caused his hands to shake. When he glanced at Andie, he saw that she looked as pale as he felt. He didn't know how to pray. Not out loud anyway. What should he do?

He was about to refuse, but an overwhelming peace gave him added confidence.

You can do this. It's time you tried.

"Yeah, sure." He folded his arms, bowed his head and closed his eyes the way he'd seen people at church do. And then he began, a simple prayer thanking the Lord for the bounty they enjoyed each day and asking for a blessing on the meal. No long speech. No frills.

When he finished, everyone lined up at the table, talking happily, enjoying the good food. No one looked at him or seemed to think his prayer too simple and unfit for the Lord.

"Well done," Brett whispered when he came to retrieve another pile of hot dogs.

"You could have warned me, brother," Matt said.

Brett shrugged his giant shoulders, his cheeks ruddy from chasing the kids. "If I had, you might have refused."

Hmm. Matt was learning not to underestimate Brett. Although he meant well, the cheerful man wasn't stupid. And Matt felt grateful to him. Without Brett, this day would have been miserable. As it was, Matt had thoroughly enjoyed himself. He felt included. Like he belonged here with his family.

"Thanks, Brett."

"No problem."

Sometime later, Matt enjoyed a hamburger and hot dog, accompanied by a heaping pile of Andie's homemade potato salad. When Andie walked by to retrieve more buns, Matt saw his chance. He let her have it. Not too much, of course. He didn't want to soak her shirt. Instead, he aimed at her legs, and she gasped as the water balloon soaked her calves and sneakers.

"Oh, you!" she gasped.

He just laughed and tossed a second balloon at her.

She yelped and jumped away, but not quickly enough. "No fair! I should've known you'd do something like this. You always get even in water fights."

A memory flashed through Matt's mind of a time when they'd gone on a river rafting trip down the Salmon River. They'd had a blast, playing in the water, camping outdoors, snapping pictures of big-horn sheep.

She ran for a water balloon, then chased him, catching him easily because he didn't try very hard to get away. Why should he run when he wanted her to catch him? Instead, he wrapped his free arm around her, clasping her throwing arm. When he tickled her ribs, her sweet laughter filled his ears. She pushed away and he let her go. What he really wanted to do was hold her tight and kiss her, but he figured little steps were better at this point in their relationship. For the first time in a long time, she'd teased him back, and his heart swelled with joy.

As she sloshed back to the pavilion, she shook her head. The smile on her face brightened Matt's day like nothing else could.

After lunch, Brett directed the kids in a game of freeze tag and red light, green light. Then they gathered the children and adults in the pavilion. Matt stood next to Andie as she lit the candles on the birthday cake. Her eyes glowed with love for their son. She began to sing "Happy Birthday," her voice high and sweet. Everyone joined in and before he thought better of it, Matt put his arm around Andie's back. It was an innocent, spontaneous gesture, but it drew the attention of the adults gathered around. Their curious gazes rested on Matt and Andie, and she tensed. Throwing water balloons at each other was different from this quiet show of affection.

Matt drew away, trying to look casual. Trying not to feel out of place or ashamed for touching his wife in public. For the first time in a long time, he'd felt like he belonged. Now he wasn't so sure. The barriers still stood between him and his wife. He couldn't read Andie anymore. One moment she was laughing and chasing him with a water balloon, the next moment she seemed to pulse with anger.

"Make a wish before you blow out the candles," Sue told Davie.

"And don't spit on the cake," Andie warned with a smile.

The boy closed his eyes and concentrated, then

opened his eyes and blew out the candles. Everyone clapped and cheered.

While Matt found a place to sit beneath a crab apple tree and rest his leg, the women served large mounds of cake. Sue brought Matt a piece and gave him a tepid smile.

"Thank you." He accepted the plate.

"You're welcome."

He picked up his fork, but she hesitated beside him and he looked up. "Is something wrong?"

She wrung her hands together, looking nervous. "I owe you an apology. I'm sorry, Matt. For everything. I deleted your messages when you called Andie a few weeks after you left. I thought you would only break her heart again. I've told her what I did. But you have to understand, she fell to pieces when you left. With a baby on the way, she didn't know what to do. You hurt her. Badly. And I just couldn't stand the thought of seeing her hurt again."

He closed his eyes for the count of two. She'd erased the evidence that he'd called Andie. That he'd made a small attempt at reconciliation. But it didn't matter anymore. Two small phone calls weren't enough to exonerate him from abandoning his wife. He should have done much more. Coming home to Andie should have been his first priority. At the very least, he should have tried to call Andie again and again until she answered, but he hadn't. He'd stopped trying.

He met Sue's gaze with all the intensity he could muster. "You needn't worry, Sue. I'll never leave Andie again, no matter what. Not ever."

"I hope not. Brett has helped me see that it's not my place to judge you. Andie's been happier since you returned, no matter what she says. I can't explain the difference. It's like she's come back to life. And I started thinking how I'd feel if I lost Brett. You can't love each other and create a child together and just look the other way. You and Andie need to work out your problems together with the Lord. I won't intercede in your marriage again."

Whew! What a large concession coming from Sue.

"I appreciate that." What else could he say? Things were difficult enough between him and Andie without him also having to fend off his sister-in-law. If God could soften Sue's heart, He could surely soften Andie.

Susan turned toward the pavilion, but then stopped, tilted her head and gave him a sidelong look. "But if you hurt my sister again, I'll hunt you down like a mangy dog."

His mouth dropped open in surprise. She simply smiled sweetly and left him there to eat his cake in silence. As he watched her go, he chuckled to himself. And then he thought about what she'd said.

Andie was happier with his return. Could it be true? Maybe he still had a chance, in spite of her anxious expressions whenever her friends were around.

Please help me, Lord. If You really exist, please help me show Andie that I'm truly sorry and deserve a second chance.

Again, his silent prayer was simple, with no embellishments. A pure expression of the desires in his heart. If only God could soften Andie's anger. If only she'd give him a second chance, he'd spend the rest of eternity striving to make her happy.

"You shouldn't have done that." Andie rolled up a plastic tablecloth before stuffing it and a pile of used paper plates and cups into a large, black garbage bag Matt held open for her.

Brett was carrying a cooler to the car while Sue had taken Rose to the restroom to change her diaper. Davie was occupied on the other end of the pavilion with his new gifts.

"Done what?" Matt asked.

She didn't look at him. "Put your arm around me or hugged me."

"We were having a water fight, sweetheart."

"And you shouldn't call me sweetheart." She continued busying herself with cleaning up. How could he have put his arm around her in front of all her friends and family? She'd seen their looks of surprised curiosity. She was tired of people asking and having to explain her relationship with Matt. And she didn't want to tell them how he'd left her years ago. Or how he'd broken her heart and then returned to her life. Instead, she'd just have to tell them it wasn't their business. She had no intention of airing her marriage problems to other people.

He placed a finger beneath her chin and tilted her face so she gazed into his eyes. "I didn't mean to embarrass you, Andie. I didn't even think before I put my arm around you. I was just having fun with my family."

She pulled away, knowing it wasn't Christian to feel angry about what he'd done, but she did. She'd had a lot of fun with him today, and she didn't want to feel this way. "That's just the problem. You didn't think. Most of my friends believe I'm divorced."

"But we're not. You're my wife, Andie."

She tried to ignore the look of sadness in his eyes, which made her feel even worse. "In name only."

"Not to me. You'll always be my dear wife."

The shattered look in his eyes wrenched her heart. For years she'd wanted nothing more than to hurt him the way he'd hurt her. Now she felt childish and ugly inside for causing him pain.

She moved away, jerking streamers of crepe paper and balloons off the wood siding of the pavilion. He shook out another garbage bag and followed her, his presence a cloying reminder of her own flaws. He didn't limp as much as usual. After a busy day of running around the park, she would have expected him to be in a lot of pain. Obviously his leg was getting better.

Who was she to criticize him when she had so many failings? He'd been trying so hard to be there for her and Davie. And yet she still couldn't find it within her heart to let him in all the way.

"I didn't mean to embarrass you, Andie." His voice carried a sincere tone she couldn't deny.

"I know. Let's just drop it, okay?"

What was wrong with her? She didn't understand. She'd made room in her life for Matt to be a father to Davie. She admitted to herself that she still cared for Matt. How could she not? She knew he wanted more, but she didn't know if she could give him that. Not now. Maybe never.

Chapter Eleven

Andie collapsed into the overstuffed chair in her living room and heaved an exhausted sigh. Thank goodness Davie's birthday came only once a year. The party in the park had gone off without a hitch and they'd had a fun time, but it'd been tiring work. She'd gratefully accepted the help of Susan, Brett and Matt.

Matt. Despite her harsh words at the end, she couldn't help smiling at the way he'd come prepared for a water fight. She should have known he'd bring a water pistol. She'd laughed so hard her sides ached. And then he'd put his arm around her. The touch of his hands on her arms ignited memories of love, which reminded her that he'd abandoned her once. She felt torn in two different directions. How could she love a man she also hated?

She stared at the pile of gifts Davie had received, most of them from Matt. A microscope, digital reader, telescope, walkie-talkies and a cookie bouquet with balloon-shaped cookies decorated with colorful frosting. All gifts from Matt.

When she and Davie had arrived home two hours earlier, they'd discovered an aquarium of fish set up in Davie's bedroom. No doubt Matt had found the spare key she kept hidden in a potted plant at the back door. He'd remembered where she kept it. He still seemed to know so much about her.

And he'd spoiled Davie rotten. To top it off, Davie had confided to her his birthday wish. He wanted his mom and daddy to get back together again.

Shaking her head, she draped an afghan over her shoulders and curled her legs beneath her. Sue had confessed about erasing Matt's phone messages years earlier. Two small phone calls. That's all. Yet it was more than she'd done. At least he'd picked up the phone and called her.

The music box he'd given her many weeks ago lay in her lap. She'd retrieved it from the top of her closet, not really knowing why she got it out. As she lifted the lid and listened to their love song, she sang along softly. Memories flooded her mind. Matt raking leaves in their front yard, working on the car and kissing her beneath the mistletoe on Christmas Eve. She missed the intimacy they'd once shared as much as the camaraderie.

When Sue had told her about the voicemails, Andie didn't have the heart to refuse her sister's apology. They all needed forgiveness. Andie didn't want to carry a grudge around in her heart against her loved ones. Not when she had so many faults of her own. Who was she to withhold her forgiveness from her family members?

From Matt?

Most of her friends now knew she and Matt were still married. Carol Gardner had been to Andie's house numerous times when she brought her son, Ronnie, over to play with Davie. The woman knew Andie and Davie lived alone. Yet Andie was still married. With her forward manner, Carol had bluntly asked Andie if she was separated from Matt. To which Andie had made a pretense of dropping a plate of food so she could pretend not to hear the question.

Andie groaned. She had no desire to answer her friends' unasked questions about her marriage to Matt. It wasn't their business.

Laying her head back against the chair, Andie picked up the remote and flipped on the TV to watch the news. She'd just put Davie to bed and realized they had church tomorrow.

Matt would probably be at church, but that didn't bother her anymore. Ever since that first difficult Sunday when Matt had shown up unexpectedly, she'd decided she kind of liked him sitting on the bench beside her and Davie. It provided a good example for Davie. It also gave Andie an odd sense of security and peace…until church ended, and she faced going home alone with Davie.

No one doubted Davie adored his daddy. The boy had even started gesturing and crossing his little legs like his father. More and more, Davie's smile and expressions reminded her of Matt. Even Sue seemed to be getting along well with him.

So why didn't Andie want to go to church? Yes, she was tired. But a good night's sleep should cure that problem.

No, this went deeper, into her soul. To her relationship with her Heavenly Father. In all honesty, Andie didn't feel worthy of God anymore. Over the years, she'd pulled away from the Lord, filling her heart with anger and self-pity. She realized she'd crowded God out, and she longed to change that. To rebuild her faith in the Lord.

It wouldn't be easy to begin. First, she'd need to ask the Lord for forgiveness. Then she'd need to forgive Matt. Even if they never got back together, she had to forgive her husband and let her anger go. She couldn't carry it around inside anymore. It'd gotten too heavy to bear. She wanted to let it go, but did she dare? If she forgave Matt, she would have to recognize that she loved him still. She'd always loved him. And that created a new dilemma.

Trust.

She would need to start trusting Matt again. Frankly, it had been more than difficult being a single mother, even with Sue's help. For years, she'd hungered for the closeness she'd once shared with her husband. She couldn't say how much she'd missed his strength and support, both emotional and physical. But how did she dare trust him enough to tell him how she felt or let him back into her heart? What assurances did she have that he wouldn't abandon her and Davie again?

None. And that scared her most of all.

"Matt, this is Andie. When you get this message, can you call me as soon as possible? I have a small problem and need your help."

Matt pressed the save button on his cell phone, then promptly dialed Andie's work number. This was a first. She needed his help.

Sitting back in his office chair, he glanced at the clock on the wall and listened to the ring tone. Two-fifteen on a Friday afternoon. Her call had come in twenty minutes ago, while he was in a staff meeting. A giddy feeling of euphoria crowded his heart. Except for the day Davie ran away, this was the first time she'd called him. What would cause her to ask him for help?

"Hello." She sounded breathless.

"Hi, Andie. It's Matt. What's up?"

"Oh, Matt. Thanks for calling back. I've been called out on a small brush fire."

He tensed, wishing she didn't have to work on

any wildfires, but knowing it was her job. "Anything serious?"

"No, but I don't have anyone to pick up Davie from school at three. Sue and Brett left town early this morning to visit his brother for a few days. Are you able to get time off work to take care of Davie—?"

"You bet. Am I on the list at school as someone who can pick him up?"

"Yes. I just went by and took care of it, so they shouldn't hassle you. But they may ask you for ID."

Wow! Maybe she was finally starting to trust him after all. "Thanks—any idea how long you'll be gone?"

"It shouldn't be more than a day. It's just two hundred acres, but you know how small fires can escalate into big ones. You can stay at my house, if that'd make things easier for you. All of Davie's clothes and toys are there. There's plenty of food. Can you fix him a decent dinner?"

"Of course. Pizza hits all the main food groups." He chuckled, unable to ignore a buzz of excitement. This was the first time she'd let him visit Davie without supervision, and he was determined not to let her down.

"I don't think so."

"Sure, pizza has pineapple, which is fruit, and onion and peppers, which are veggies."

"Davie will just pick all of that off. How about adding a can of string beans?"

"I was thinking about eating in a restaurant. Will the salad bar work if I talk him into eating some carrots?"

She hesitated before relenting. "Well, it is a Friday night. I'm sure Davie would love to get pizza with his daddy."

He caught a bit of humor in her tone and couldn't help feeling like they'd made a lot of headway today. He was going to enjoy a boys' night out with his son. "Don't worry, Andie. I'll take good care of our boy."

She paused. "If you have an emergency, our list of doctors is on the corkboard by the phone in the kitchen. They have my insurance information on file. I've got to go."

"Okay. And Andie? You take care out there, will you? I want you to come home safe."

"Of course."

"Good. I'll see you when you get home."

"Bye."

He waited for her to hang up before he did so. He'd wanted to tell her he loved her, but figured that was pushing things. He didn't want her to go. A feeling of absolute terror clogged his chest, making it difficult to breathe. What if something went wrong? What if she were hurt out there?

As it was, he couldn't wait to pick up Davie. Looking at the clock again, he realized he had just enough time to finish the report he'd been working on, let Cal and the front receptionist know why he was taking off a bit early today, then drive over to Davie's school.

Maybe they'd catch a movie tonight. He wondered what was playing at the theater in town. If it was a grown-up picture, he might take Davie over to the video rental store to pick up something for kids. If all else failed, pizza and a baseball game always hit the spot. He'd been working hard on the treadmill and figured he could afford one day off from his exercises to spend time with his son. His work-capacity test was in two weeks and he'd be ready.

After turning off his computer, he walked outside to the parking lot. No cane. Barely a limp. Not much pain. Truly God had blessed him in his recovery. He felt euphoric, like he could conquer the world. The Lord had performed a miracle for him, bringing him home to his family. Now if he could just forget about the wildfire and win over Andie, he'd be a happy man.

The drive to Davie's school took less than ten minutes. He arrived just as the final bell rang. Inside the office, he reported to the receptionist.

"So you're Davie's father. Your wife told us you'd be by. Let me call Davie for you." She picked up the phone and dialed what Matt assumed must be Davie's kindergarten room.

Had Andie told the receptionist she was his wife? Or was the receptionist assuming? He almost asked, but didn't want to create fodder for gossip.

Matt stepped over by the door to wait. He felt nervous, unable to get Andie off his mind. He hated the thought that she might be hurt on the wildfire. He flipped open his cell phone, thinking to call her just to check in, but knew now wasn't the time to distract her from her job. She was a highly trained professional and knew what she was doing. But he'd been highly trained also, and look where that had gotten him.

No, he couldn't bother her right now. He pocketed his phone, determined to be patient. But he couldn't help saying a silent prayer and holding it there in his heart until she came home safe.

Children swarmed the hallway, some dragging their jackets behind them, others carrying lunch pails and books. Their happy chatter filled the hall. It felt odd, yet comfortable to be in a school waiting for his son.

"Dad!"

Matt turned as Davie launched into his arms. At the age of six, Davie wasn't embarrassed by hugs and kisses. Yet.

Matt squeezed his son, enjoying the show of physical affection while he could. "Hi, hotshot. How was school today?"

"Great! Where's Mom?" He wore his jacket zipped up to his chin and carried a handful of papers with his name scrawled at the top along with smiley faces and gold stars.

Davie took Matt's hand as they walked outside.

"She's been called out on a wildfire, so she asked me to pick you up. How do you feel about pizza and a movie tonight?"

"Yeah!" Davie punched the air with his free hand.

The rest of the evening was indescribable for Matt. They laughed, ate pizza and ice cream, played video games and watched a movie. True to his word, Matt ensured Davie ate three carrot sticks and several wedges of apple. Davie fell asleep snuggled beneath a blanket against Matt's side on the couch in Andie's living room. Right where Matt wanted to be.

Around midnight, Matt carried Davie to his bed. In spite of the fatigue weighing his body, Matt's mind remained active. For some reason, Andie being on a wildfire troubled him more than he could say. What if the winds changed and she was caught in the fire? All sorts of horrific scenarios played out in his mind, making him shake with fear. He couldn't lose her. Not now. Not ever.

His thoughts returned to the wildfire that had taken the life of his crewman. Night had become his enemy, haunting him with what had happened and what he should have done differently.

In spite of the cool night air, sweat beaded on his brow and his hands trembled. How he wished Andie was home safe instead of out fighting fire.

He prowled the house, feeling closer to Andie as he skimmed his fingers across her bottles of perfume, hairbrush and pictures of her laughing with their son. Someday he hoped she included pictures of him on top of her dresser. As he concentrated on these tangible items, he was able to calm his troubled mind. Surprised appreciation filled him when he saw the music box he'd given to her sitting on the nightstand beside her bed. At least she hadn't thrown it away.

In the bathroom, he noticed the laundry basket filled with dirty clothes. Andie worked hard. Since he couldn't sleep, maybe he could make himself useful.

Picking up the basket, he carried it to the laundry room and started a load of clothes in the washer. By 3:00 a.m., he'd completed two loads and finally felt drowsy. Out of respect for his wife, he opted to sleep on the couch.

Davie awakened him once in the night, asking for a glass of water. While Matt got a cup, the boy stood in his pajamas and bare feet in the glow of the night-light and rubbed his weary eyes. Matt's heart squeezed. How he loved this innocent child. How he loved his beautiful wife for giving him this wonderful gift.

"Here you go, sweetheart." Matt handed the cup to the boy, then rubbed Davie's back while he gulped the water down.

Davie handed the cup back to Matt and murmured sleepily, "Thanks, Dad."

The boy turned and padded back to his room

with Matt following. After Davie climbed into bed, Matt covered him up with a blanket and kissed his forehead.

"Daddy?"

Matt paused at the door, peering at his son through the dark. "Yes, son?"

"I'm glad you're here." Davie yawned and rolled over, his gentle breathing filling the silence.

Matt stood frozen, too overcome by emotion to speak for several moments. Finally he whispered, "I'm glad I'm here, too."

He returned to the couch where he offered a silent prayer of gratitude, then instantly fell asleep. Both he and Davie slept late. In the morning, Matt made pancakes for breakfast. Davie helped Matt wash the dishes and do other chores around the house. Matt had never had so much fun cleaning the bathrooms.

Davie grinned as he swirled the brush around in the toilet bowl. "Won't Mom be surprised when she sees what we've done?" With his little hands, Davie wasn't very thorough, but Matt thought it important to let him help with the work.

"I think she will." Matt squirted cleanser into the sink before scrubbing it and then the bathtub. When they finished, he made sure both he and Davie washed their hands good before hanging out fresh towels.

After dusting and running the vacuum, Matt finished folding the laundry. Davie had taken up residence on the couch where he fell asleep watching a kid's program. The late night before and the chores today had tired him out. The child was there when Andie came home, her ranger uniform smudged with soot and smelling of wood smoke.

"Hi," she greeted Matt with a whisper when she saw Davie sleeping.

She set her fire pack on the floor before gazing at her son, a soft smile gracing her appealing lips. Even with her hair pulled back in a long ponytail and covered with grime, Matt thought her beautiful. Her eyes were bloodshot from smoke and creased with fatigue.

"Hi there. You look tired." Matt squelched the urge to kiss her hello. It seemed a natural response, but he doubted she'd approve. He had to keep reminding himself that he was only babysitting. He didn't live here. He still didn't belong.

She let out a big sigh. "I am tired."

They moved into the kitchen where they could talk without waking Davie. Matt got her a tall glass of ice water.

"Thanks. How did things go?" She took a sip, her gaze scanning the table where clean laundry lay folded in tidy piles.

"Great. We had a blast together."

"You washed my laundry?" Her eyes widened.

He shrugged. "I hope it's okay. I figured I'd make myself useful while I was here."

She glanced around the room and sniffed. "I smell pine."

"I mopped the floors."

From the doorway, her gaze scanned the living room. "And you vacuumed, too."

"And took out the garbage, dusted and scoured out the bathrooms. Davie helped, of course."

"Wow! Thanks for being here when I needed you, Matt. I really appreciate it." She stepped close and kissed him on the mouth, a quick hit-and-run kiss that startled both of them.

When she stepped back, her eyes widened with horror, as if just realizing what she'd done. And then he knew. She felt it, too. The comfortable atmosphere, the spontaneous actions and instinctive relationship they'd shared years earlier. The physical attraction. It was all coming back to them, yet she continued to fight it.

"I'm sure glad you're home safe." He'd been so worried about her, pacing the floor, checking the clock. Fearing the worst. Now he could stop fretting. She was fine.

A feeling of jubilation swept him. The chemistry between them was still there. It hadn't died. Not in all these long, lonely years apart. Surely she still felt something more for him besides hate and anger. Dare he hope she might still love him, at least a little?

She moved away, running her fingertips across the clean countertop and sink. During their marriage, he'd rarely thanked her for cleaning their house, washing their clothes and preparing meals. Why did he deserve her gratitude now when she always did these things without a word from him?

"I never thanked you for taking such good care of our home, Andie. I have a greater appreciation for you now. You were a great wife, and I should have told you every day how much I appreciated the many things you did for me."

She glanced at him, an endearing smudge of dirt across her chin. "You thanked me sometimes."

"Not enough. I took you for granted. I'm sorry for that."

She noticed the toolbox sitting beside the back door and nodded at it. "What else have you been up to?"

"Davie helped me repair the gate in the backyard. I showed him how the latch works and how to fix it. I thought he was old enough to start learning how to take care of those things."

She glanced out the kitchen window, her mouth dropping open. "That gate has been troubling me for several weeks. I thought I'd have all these chores waiting for me when I got home, and I'm so tired I really don't feel up to it. You've taken care of everything."

His heart swelled with joy. "It was my pleasure. After you get cleaned up, I hope you can just rest. I'm so glad you're home safe."

She looked at his legs. "You're walking without your cane more and more."

A smile spread its way across his face. He couldn't help it. He hated the cane and didn't miss it one bit. "I'm happy to say I've given it up for good. On Thursday, I hiked three miles in forty-five minutes wearing a forty-five-pound pack."

She gasped. "You passed the arduous level of the wildfire physical?"

He nodded. "Not officially, but I'll take the test during our fire-training school in two weeks."

"Oh, Matt. I know that must have been so hard. It's wonderful." She rested a hand on his arm, her eyes filled with genuine happiness for his accomplishment.

Tremors of awareness shot up his arm. He looked down, then gazed into her eyes and stepped closer. His hands lifted of their own volition, twining around her arms. Pulling her closer. She didn't fight him. Didn't look away or try to avoid him. She gazed into his eyes, her mouth softened with a smile. Maybe she could finally forgive him. Maybe—

"Hi, Mommy!" Davie startled them apart.

"Davie! Oh, I missed you." Andie knelt before her son and hugged him tight.

He pulled back, his nose crinkling with distaste. "You're squashing my eye and you stink."

Andie laughed. "I smell like a fire, right?"

"Yes."

"That's because I've been fighting a wildfire."

"You need a bath," Davie said.

"And a change of clothes," she agreed with a laugh.

Taking her cue, Matt stepped toward the door. He ruffled Davie's hair as he passed by. "And I need to do my exercises. I'll be going now. See you around, hotshot."

"Ah, can't you stay? Do you have to go?" Davie asked.

"Afraid so."

"But why can't you just live here with us?"

Matt didn't respond, but his gaze locked with Andie's. An expression of confusion and embarrassment crossed her face, her eyes filled with dread. The physical closeness they'd just shared had taken them both off guard. Now her defenses seemed to have gone back up. He released a deep sigh, knowing she still wasn't ready to forgive him.

Andie accompanied him out onto the front porch, her arms folded across her dirty forest ranger shirt. "Will you be at church tomorrow?"

He turned on the first step, holding the railing, wishing he could stay. "Yes. Are you worried I might embarrass you?"

She hesitated, then shook her head. He saw sincerity in her eyes. "No, I was just wondering when we'd see you again."

He smiled. "That's good. Because I sure want to see *you* again."

She turned her head and stared at the grass, her mouth tight. Her shoulders tensed, as if she were about to step off a precipice and fall on the sharp rocks far below. "Sue and Brett are out of town. Why don't you plan to come over here for Sunday dinner? Davie would like that, and I owe you for all the work you did here at home."

A long breath escaped his lungs. Finally. Finally she'd invited him over of her own free will. "I gladly accept, but you owe me nothing, babe. Nothing at all. I'm just trying to take care of my family the best way I know how."

"I'll see you tomorrow." Her face filled with color, and she turned and went back inside.

As Matt walked to his truck, his chuckle turned into happy laughter. He'd called her babe and she hadn't chastised him for it. Just before climbing inside his truck, he raised his hands in the air and yelled, "Yes!"

They'd made substantial headway. She'd trusted him alone with Davie and invited him over for dinner. If only he could forget the nightmares still plaguing him. If only...

He hated thinking about the wildfire, but couldn't help it. How he wished it hadn't happened. If only he hadn't lost radio contact with the lookout. He should have been more vigilant. More careful.

And yet, the wildfire had brought him back home to Andie and his son. It had set him on a path to God. He couldn't regret the closeness he'd developed with the Lord over the past months. But how could he reconcile what had happened with Jim? He was gone and Matt could never bring him back.

A forlorn ache deep in his soul told him he could never be completely happy again until he resolved the guilt he felt over losing his crewman. He longed for Jim's forgiveness and felt bereft, knowing he might never have it.

Chapter Twelve

"You're early." Matt smiled at Andie when she arrived at Taylor Park at 6:00 a.m. on Monday morning.

"I figured you could use the extra help. We've got a lot to do today. How many recruits will we be training this week?" An air of excitement pulsed through her veins as she breathed in the crisp morning air. She tried to tell herself it was because of the many training events she would be teaching and had nothing to do with the handsome man standing beside her.

"About three hundred and fifty new recruits and another eighty men and women needing recertification in various aspects of wildfire fighting."

Dressed in spruce-green Nomex pants and a yellow wildfire-fighting shirt, she'd pulled her hair back in a ponytail to keep it out of her eyes. With her sunglasses perched atop her head, she folded her Nomex gloves securely inside one of the wide cargo pockets on her pants.

Even at this hour, people milled around the park, folding up bedrolls, dressed in a variety of exercise shorts and firefighting gear. At least seventy tents sat in tidy rows across the grass where trainees had slept the night before. Many recruits had opted to stay in the local motel or were driving in from the surrounding towns.

"You've done a great job organizing this training event. I can see this took a lot of effort." She couldn't help admiring Matt's hard work. She'd attended trainings where everyone ran around in confusion. But not today. She'd forgotten how good Matt was at his job.

Matt chuckled, the dimple in his cheek deepening. "I figure if I feed everyone well, they'll overlook possible moments of chaos. I've got a good logistics chief."

She understood his reasoning. Crew members frequently expended up to six thousand calories per day fighting wildfire. Crews had to be fed well or they'd start collapsing with heat exhaustion and overwork.

Catering trailers with exterior counters and wide roll-up windows stood in the east parking lot. Picnic tables sat close by where hordes of recruits chatted and ate a hearty breakfast of biscuits and gravy, hot cereals, pancakes, eggs, juice, bacon and sausage.

Rows of portable toilets and trailers with showers lined the inner perimeter of the west parking lot. Eight yellow school buses able to carry sixty-five people each waited along the edge of the road. The buses would transport the recruits up the mountain to the staging area where crews of twenty men and women would start a controlled burn. By the end of the week, all trainees would participate in hands-on wildfire fighting or be recertified in map and pumper-truck work.

Before anything else, new recruits and people like Matt would either pass their work capacity test or not. Those who didn't succeed would be counseled to return home, train a few more weeks, and try again later. Firefighters who couldn't keep up during an emergency evacuation endangered the lives of every person on their crew. They must be physically fit.

"You ready for your physical?" From beneath lowered lashes, Andie admired Matt's lean, strong body dressed in workout clothes. He wore a radio chest harness across his white T-shirt for communication purposes, light blue sweatpants and sneakers.

"I am. I've been warming up for an hour. I can't wait to finish this. I trained in my wildland fire boots, knowing they were heavier. I thought it'd give me an edge during the real test."

From his animated expression, she realized passing the work capacity test wasn't just about being fit enough to fight wildfire. It also represented a great victory of rehabilitating his body after a tragic event that had nearly cost his life.

"Matt, I—I'm proud of you." The concession came hard for her, but she couldn't help admiring the indomitable man she'd married. In spite of the adversity he'd faced, he'd come back fighting harder than ever. He was trying so hard to make things right. Maybe she shouldn't make it so difficult for him.

"I appreciate that. Your approval means everything to me."

She returned his smile. "You've earned it."

"Well, I didn't come in with a lot of time to spare three days ago when I hiked the course. I'm a bit nervous about finishing in time."

His confession softened her. She doubted he'd confide such a thing to anyone else. The fact that he'd told her made her feel closer to him. Like a special confidant he trusted with his deepest secrets. Memories of the closeness they'd once shared filled her mind. They used to tell each other everything. When he'd returned to her life a few months ago, she hadn't wanted to know anything about him. Now she couldn't help cheering for him. How could that be?

They walked together to the command station, a long trailer that had been brought in and set up with maps, phones, desks and computers. Matt showed not a hint of a limp, moving with his old sleek grace. Seeing him in this environment made Andie feel all warm inside. She loved this man in a uniform. She always had. He appeared so strong and in control. Like the man she'd married years earlier, only different. This man seemed to be all of the good she'd hoped for and none of the bad. He'd changed and evolved into a considerate, caring, confident man who knew what he wanted and went after it with gusto.

A surge of pride enveloped Andie's chest. Approximately four hundred and fifty recruits from the Nevada Department of Forestry, the Forest Service and the Bureau of Land Management were participating in the week-long schedule.

Since she'd already passed the arduous level of the physical fitness, Andie would teach fire safety, fire-line construction, and serve as a timer on the fitness course.

She glanced at Matt, noticing he'd gotten his hair cut high and tight again, like a U.S. Marine going into battle. "You know, as the Operations Section Chief, you're only required to pass the medium-level physical."

"I know."

"Then why push yourself so hard?"

"First, because I won't ask something of my crews that I can't do myself. Second, because I hate walking with a cane. I knew if I could pass the arduous level, I'd rehabilitate my legs. It's hurt like a mother bear, but I made it. No more cane."

His voice carried a lilting quality that showed his happiness and relief. Easy to understand. And yet, any ordinary man would have settled for less.

With the help of ten trainers directing foot traffic, Matt used a megaphone to call the recruits to the buses. Some would begin classroom training while others would pass their physicals. Those recertifying on skills such as chainsaws and tree felling would accompany specific trainers.

The ride up the mountain took over an hour. As he directed the recruits and delegated responsibilities, Matt seemed tense, constantly looking at his watch. Andie figured he'd be nervous until he passed his test.

By the time they arrived at the fitness course, Andie took the lead. Using Matt's megaphone, she called out instructions to the first group of men and women eager to pass their physical training.

"You have fifteen minutes to warm up before we begin. Then you will line up in rows of six across. The number pinned to your shirt will tell us who you are, so don't lose it."

She paused while everyone stretched and strapped on their weight vests before lining up in neat rows. A scale was used to weigh each person's vest, to ensure they started and ended with the appropriate amount of weight for their specific training level. Then Andie began the test.

"Welcome. You are about to take a job-related work capacity test to determine your fitness for duty."

She continued reading from a script, to ensure she didn't miss any instructions. Three out of the five days of training would include national standardized training. Through the crowd of recruits, she caught sight of Matt standing with several highly trained professionals who also needed to renew their physical certification. Matt listened carefully, his jaw locked, his face tight with concentration.

She continued. "Jogging or running will result in disqualification. You are free to stop at any time for any reason, but you must finish the course within forty-five minutes. A walking staff may be used. Are there any questions?"

A young recruit that looked fresh out of high school raised his hand.

"Yes?" Andie gazed at him.

"Can we carry water with us?"

"Absolutely, but it is not included in the forty-five pounds of your weight vest."

Another hand shot up, and Andie nodded at the young woman.

"Are we allowed to remove our weight vest during the course?"

"No. You should already know that. Your vest will be weighed at the end of the course. If it doesn't weigh exactly forty-five pounds, you will be disqualified. We have spotters along the course to ensure your safety, but also to ensure the integrity of the test. So leave your vest on and do your best. This isn't a race against anyone but yourself. Are there any more questions?"

A hush fell over the group.

"Okay, Rick Olton will get you started." She nodded at Rick, then left to climb aboard a four-wheeler and drive up the mountain where she took her position at the halfway mark.

Holding a stopwatch in one hand and a clipboard in the other, she stood at the side of the course and waited. As the test administrator, she had the right to consider terminating candidates who were substantially behind the required pace. Though she hoped everyone passed their physical, she knew she'd have to be tough on those who couldn't. Being lenient would only endanger lives once the recruits were deployed to an actual wildfire incident.

For some reason, she felt jittery inside. It meant a lot to her that Matt succeed with his goals and pass this test. That puzzled her. His career had stolen their marriage. So why did she care if he passed his physical?

The answer came clear as a fire bell. She cared because it was important to him. Because she loved him, no matter how hard she tried not to. And when you loved someone, you cared about them. Their happiness and sorrows became your own.

Within twenty minutes, trainees started passing by, most of them quite young and in superb physical condition. Andie called out their time, scanning them for signs of duress or cheating. Spotters were assigned responsibility for specific recruits and identified them by the number pinned to the trainees' shirts. As the recruits passed by, the spotters glanced at the numbers pinned to each person's shirt, then jotted notes on their clipboards under that specific person's name.

Andie couldn't believe the endurance of some of the recruits. They were strong. Even though she could easily pass this course, she was now thirty-two years old and envied the stamina of the younger trainees.

"Keep one foot on the ground at all times. No running," she called to a trainee who was almost jogging. The kid immediately slowed his pace to a fast hike.

Matt approached, walking fast, his muscular arms pumping, his face tense. Seeing him made Andie's heart beat faster, and she couldn't help smiling.

"Looking good, hotshot." The moment she said the words, she regretted them. What if he mistook her meaning?

His glittering eyes met her gaze and he nodded

once, but didn't break stride. She resisted the urge to watch him pass, forcing herself to focus on the other trainees coming up the trail. Silently, she cheered Matt on.

Come on, honey. You can do this.

She instantly regretted her line of thinking. She'd called him honey, not out loud, but the sentiment was there just the same. He spent so much time over at her house that she'd gotten comfortable around him.

Too comfortable.

She shook her head, forcing herself to focus on the chore at hand. Within forty-five minutes, eleven recruits were still on the course. Andie stopped them long enough to give them a pep talk about training harder and returning once they could pass the course.

"We'll be offering another physical in three weeks. Call my office for details." She handed each one her card. "That'll give you enough time to build up more endurance and still join a summer fire crew. Don't give up. Don't quit. You're almost there."

One overweight man caused Andie a bit of concern. The recruit's face flushed red, his breath wheezing from his mouth like a tea kettle at full boil. The number one cause of death on wildfires was heart attack, and Andie feared she might have to perform CPR on the man.

"Let's walk it back to the starting line nice and slow," she said.

She longed to race ahead to find out how Matt had done on the course. Instead, she remained with the out-of-shape recruit until certain he was safely on a bus making its way down the mountain.

Andie found Matt at the buses, signing task books for each job the recruits had completed and directing them so they knew where they needed to be for their next class. He'd changed into his forest service uniform, and his face glowed with contentment. Without asking, she knew he'd passed his physical.

"Hey! Come here," Matt called out to a new recruit. The young man stopped and walked over to Matt, who reached forward and took the hand tool the kid had been carrying on his shoulder.

"Packing this Pulaski like that is a recipe for getting hurt." The Pulaski was a hand tool that combined an ax and an adze into one head and aided firefighters in digging soil or chopping wood.

The young man's eyes filled with uncertainty.

"What if you trip over this rough terrain?" Matt asked the kid. "You could cut your own throat carrying that ax up by your head. Believe me, I've seen it happen before. Instead, always carry sharp tools at your downhill side, grip the handle firmly near the head and point the ax end away from your body toward the ground like this." Matt modeled the proper way to carry the tool.

The recruit watched carefully, then nodded. "Okay, I got it. Sorry."

Matt handed the tool back and showed a warm smile, softening his rebuff. "Nothing to be sorry about. You're here to learn. Over the next few days, we're gonna teach you a whole lot more. You'll be a trained wildfire fighter by the time we're finished with you."

The trainee smiled, seeming to like that idea. "Thanks, sir."

Matt clapped the young man once on the back. "You're welcome."

The recruit carried the hand tool as directed, a new air of confidence in his step as he climbed on the bus. Andie never doubted the importance of these interactive classroom exercises and incident settings. It was the best way to teach recruits.

"So? How'd you do on your physical?" Andie asked casually as she passed by Matt on her way to her next training assignment.

A euphoric grin creased his handsome mouth. "I passed with six minutes to spare. No more cane, ever."

"I never had any doubt," she called over her shoulder.

But she did have doubts. About his mental well-being and about his motives for coming back into her life.

As the week of training continued, the recruits were broken out into twenty-member crews. They started out by learning the organization and hierarchy of firefighting. Andie found herself amazed by Matt's skill both as a firefighter and as a teacher. He knew so much and had so much to offer that she could no longer begrudge him his career. He'd earned every bit of his success. Now they needed to work on their family life.

Each crew was taken up on the mountain where they learned to work with hoses and hand pumps, and how to clear fuels and limbs off trees as they built fire line. Trainees created fires with drip torches, learning to start controlled burns. Small bombs were lit and tossed into the fire to flare up and create more depth in the fire.

Matt directed the trainees through the motions of what to do when they arrived first on the scene of a wildfire. Working together with Rick Olton and Hank Corbridge, Matt showed the recruits how to take direct action to slow down the fire and then begin to mop up afterward. In essence, the students took the knowledge they had learned in the classroom and put it into action out in the field. And in the process, they cleared a lot of dead wood and other debris off the mountain that could easily catch fire during a lightning storm.

Andie's fears for Matt's mental health were confirmed when they taught a safety workshop together. Andie hadn't asked to teach this class with Matt, but she'd found her name on the roster when the final assignments were handed out.

Standing outside in a clearing surrounded by dried grass, Matt began his lecture. "Every time a tragedy occurs, it's because one of the ten standard firefighting orders or one of the eighteen watchout situations was disobeyed." Matt hesitated at the front of the class, his voice trembling slightly. "Above all else..." He coughed and began again. "Above all else, communication is of critical importance. When an order is given, you should... you should repeat it back to ensure you understand completely. Misunderstanding an order can cost lives."

He stepped back and reached for his fire shelter. "Never, ever remove your fire shelter from your fire pack. If you ever need to deploy your shelter, pick the largest available clearing you can find and avoid anything that might burn. Wear your gloves and hard hat, and a face and neck shroud if you have one handy."

He clasped the fire shelter in his hands before pulling the red ring to tear off the plastic bag. Holding the grasp handles, he shook the shelter hard to fold it out. And then he froze, standing like a statue. At first, Andie thought he was gathering his thoughts. Then she tilted her head and saw his expression. He stared down at the shelter, terror filling his eyes. He shivered, as if haunting memories washed over him. It only lasted a few moments before he regained control, but not before she saw his crippling fear.

Oh, no! He wasn't over the wildfire. In spite of claiming differently and rehabilitating his legs, he hadn't fully recovered.

"Matt." She touched his arm and he looked at her, his expression blank. Gone was the strong, confident firefighter, replaced by a mere mortal man.

No! Not here. Not now. If anyone suspected he still had this problem, it could prove catastrophic to his career. She had to help him. Had to protect him.

She wrenched the shelter free of his hands and continued the demonstration, acting like nothing had happened. "You will climb into your shelter and lie facedown. Place your legs toward the on-coming fire and bury your mouth near the dirt. The air can be hot enough to burn your lungs, but the air near the ground is coolest. Use your gloved hand to keep from inhaling dirt, but protect your lungs as much as possible."

"And…and you must withstand the pain at all costs." Matt's eyes appeared lucid, but haunted. "The pain may be so great from the heat that you think you're dying. Your natural instinct will be to get out and run. But I guarantee if you climb out of your shelter, you…you will die. Stay where you are. It's your only chance for survival. I know…I know this firsthand."

Andie's heart wrenched. Without intending to, he'd just revealed a lot about the wildfire. She could only imagine what he'd gone through. How hard it must have been. And still he'd survived.

Why? Why had Matt survived when his man had died? Was it a simple matter of greater physical strength and endurance? Or was it something more divine? Surely the Lord had been there with Matt and the other man. Perhaps God had wanted Matt to live, so he could learn a lesson about faith.

And then a new thought occurred to her. Maybe God had spared Matt's life so he could return to her and Davie. She'd been so angry at Matt that she hadn't stopped to think that God still loved and cared for him. The Lord never abandoned any of His children, no matter what they did. Had God saved Matt's life for a greater purpose?

"Rick, will you review the organization of the Incident Command System one more time? Once you're done, we can move on to the tool-handling workshop." Taking the lead, Andie nodded at Rick Olton before drawing Matt away from the group where they could talk in private.

"I'm okay, Andie." He lifted a hand to interrupt her before she could even speak.

She caught the scent of wood smoke from one of the fires built by another training crew and lowered her voice so no one would overhear. "Well, you don't look okay to me."

"I just had a moment, that's all."

"A moment of what, Matt? I saw your face. You

looked horrified. You're not okay, no matter what you think."

He ducked his head, his expression filled with angry grief. "I was just remembering. It took me off guard, that's all. Everything was just fine and then…I'm not sure what happened."

"That's because it's still lurking inside of you."

"Not when I'm with you and Davie. Then I can forget for a time."

"Forget what?"

He shrugged, a deep abiding melancholy filling his eyes. "That I survived."

"Oh, Matt. You've got to let it go. I have no doubt your crewman wouldn't want you to torture yourself like this. He'd want you to live and be happy. He'd tell you to cherish every minute of your life."

"I'm trying, Andie. I'm trying to make a new life with new priorities, but it's so hard when—"

He didn't need to finish his statement. She knew what he was going to say. It was hard when she kept him beyond arm's reach and wouldn't let him back in. She needed to do some deep soul searching of her own, but not here and now.

"And what if you freeze up like that on a real wildfire?" she said. "You could get yourself and others killed."

His face darkened. "Don't you think I know that?"

"Then do something about it. You need to visit a

professional doctor. This is eating you up inside, I can see that. You need to talk about this, Matt. It's not going away just because you want it to. You're going to have to deal with it."

"I said I'm okay and I meant it." His voice lowered to a dangerous growl and his eyes narrowed. His strong, stubborn chin seemed chiseled out of granite.

He looked at her like she was his enemy, which wasn't true. She wished him no harm, and she knew he knew it. He was still hurting inside. Hurting and angry, just like her, except for different reasons. But her anger wouldn't get her or other people killed. His anger could.

There were worse things in life than physical death. Such as the death of a soul. And right at that moment, Andie feared for Matt's soul. If he didn't find a way to deal with his anguish, she feared he might be lost for good. She might never be able to reach him. Not if the Lord couldn't reach him first.

"Matt, I just want to help—"

"Leave it alone, Andie. It's not your worry," he snapped.

She took a step back, surprised at the dark glare on his face. Even before he'd left her, she'd never seen him so angry.

"Matt—"

He turned and walked away, cutting her off.

She stared after him, wishing for the first time in more than six years that he'd let her in. He'd shut her off just like she'd been shutting him out, and it didn't feel good. He'd always been self-contained and a master at concealing his deeper emotions, but now she didn't think it was healthy.

Maybe it was time they reconciled. Maybe she'd been too hard on Matt. Everyone carried sorrow inside of them that the eye couldn't see. Matt was no exception. And she hated the thought that he was hurting inside, and she couldn't help him.

Yes, it was time to put the broken pieces of their marriage back together. But how? How could they ever reconcile when he still carried the horror of the wildfire deep inside of him? She couldn't see a way. The only weapon she had now was prayer.

Chapter Thirteen

"What're you doing, hotshot?" Matt greeted Davie as he sauntered up the sidewalk leading to Andie's front porch.

The hot June weather had brought with it a plethora of blooming flowers, fragrant air, and dry lightning storms that cracked across the Ruby Mountains that skirted the edge of town. Matt didn't limp at all, enjoying the renewed confidence he felt with not having to walk with a cane.

The boy turned, his eyes round with surprise. "Hi, Daddy! I'm putting out a forest fire."

Davie waved, but remained where he stood at the side of the lawn. Holding the garden hose with both hands, he sprayed a stream of water at the lilac bush. He wore Andie's white firefighter helmet and yellow Nomex shirt, the sleeves pushed back on his little arms and the overlong tail dragging across the grass.

Matt chuckled. A feeling of pleasure coursed

through his veins when he thought of his son following in his footsteps and becoming a wildfire fighter. Then Matt thought better of it. The last thing he wanted was for his son to be endangered by a forest fire.

Stepping to the faucet, Matt turned the water off with a few quick twists of his wrist.

"Hey! What'd you do that for?" Davie squawked.

"We've got better things to do right now." Matt scooped the boy into his arms, and Davie dropped the hose as Matt headed toward the door.

The helmet slid down to cover Davie's face, and he pushed it back before looking into his father's eyes. He grinned when he noticed the dark suit Matt was wearing and the bouquet of red roses he held in one hand. "Are those flowers for Mom? What're you all dressed up for?"

Matt set Davie on his feet before they stepped inside the house. "You'll find out soon enough."

A tremor of excitement ran up Matt's spine. He just hoped Andie wouldn't be angry with him. When he'd called her earlier, she'd been outside weeding the garden. Davie had taken the cordless phone to her. Matt had casually asked if she had any plans for her Saturday, and she'd said just chores. She should be cleaned up by now. It was late afternoon and he hoped she wouldn't resist what he had in mind.

"Well, this is a surprise." She stood in the hallway wearing comfy blue jeans, her long hair slightly damp from a recent washing and hanging in loose waves around her shoulders. Her gaze swept over him, taking in his immaculate suit, white shirt and tie. And the roses.

Her gaze lifted to his face. "What's going on?"

Davie stood beside him, wriggling as he waited for Matt to explain. "It's May thirtieth."

"And?" Her eyes flooded with tears and she blinked her eyes.

From her sudden emotion, Matt realized she knew exactly what today was. He met her halfway down the hall and handed her the roses. "Happy anniversary, sweetheart."

Leaning forward, he placed a gentle kiss on her forehead. She didn't pull away—a good sign. He longed to take her into his arms, but still didn't dare. For so long now, he'd tried not to push her too fast, but he was reaching the point where he wished she'd either forgive him or tell him to get lost forever. This middle-of-the-road stuff almost drove him crazy.

"It's been ten years today. I—I wanted to forget." Her voice trembled.

"I know. We haven't had a lot to celebrate. Until now."

His gaze locked with hers. Emotion bubbled over inside him, and he bit his tongue to keep from telling her all the love he felt within his heart. "I'd like to take us all out for dinner, if that's okay. I wanted to surprise you. I've made reservations."

Her mouth dropped open, an equal mixture of regret and defensiveness written across her face.

His stomach clenched. He'd made her cry too many times. "You're not gonna make a liar out of me again, are you?"

She sniffed. "What do you mean?"

"I promised myself I'd never make you cry again, but you're looking mighty close to tears right now. I'd much rather see one of your sweet smiles."

She laughed and tilted her head to one side, her eyes immediately drying. "But I don't have anyone to watch Davie."

Matt shrugged. "Good, because I planned to take him with us."

"Yay!" The boy jumped up and down. "Let's go, Mom. Come on!"

She glanced back and forth between Davie and Matt while she bit her bottom lip. Oh, no! Matt knew that look. It meant she was inclined to refuse.

"Okay, but I have to change first. I'll be back." She headed toward her bedroom.

Matt exhaled a sharp breath of relief. "Take your time. We're in no hurry tonight."

The minute she disappeared, Davie raced to his room and quickly reappeared carrying his white shirt and little tie. The shirt looked rather crumpled, but the child had already pulled his T-shirt over his head and was reaching for the white shirt before Matt could speak. It was on the edge of his tongue to tell Davie he didn't need to dress up. But then Matt thought better. It was good that Davie learn young to show respect to his future wife by dressing up and treating her well. Six months ago, Matt had no idea he had a son. Now he was delighted to be teaching his boy some good behaviors. And yet, Matt had no doubt he'd also teach Davie a few bad lessons, as well. The important thing was to keep trying and never give up.

"We're gonna look nice for Mom tonight, huh?" Davie said.

"Yes, son, we will." Matt smiled, loving this boy and his wife so much that his heart ached with it.

He sat on the couch, helping Davie adjust the tie. "Why don't you bring your comb, and I'll help you with your hair."

Davie did as asked. Then they waited. The kid's show on TV put Matt to sleep within ten minutes. When Andie woke him up half an hour later with a gentle touch on his shoulder, he jerked and blinked his eyes.

A vision of loveliness stood before him, and his mouth almost watered. Andie, wearing a shapely red dress with four-inch-high heels, her makeup in place and curled hair swirling around her shoulders. Was she real? Or a dream?

He stood up fast and inhaled deeply. "Wow! You look beautiful. And you smell nice, too."

"Yeah, Mom. You smell real nice," Davie interjected.

She looked down at her son, her long lashes

resting against her pale cheeks. "Sorry to take so long."

Matt's ears buzzed with happiness. She'd dressed up. For him. When he'd come here tonight, he'd expected anger and resentment. Not this lovely apparition standing before him. "It was well worth the wait."

She stepped toward the door, carrying a small, glittering handbag. "Shall we go?"

Matt hurried around her to get the door. "Allow me, sweetheart."

Sweetheart.

Words of endearment just seemed to sneak out of his mouth spontaneously, an unconscious expression of what was in his heart. He found himself peering at her face, awaiting her look of disapproval. When it didn't come, he grew bolder, holding her arm as he led her to his truck. He'd almost forgotten about Davie until he felt the warmth of his son's small hand slip into his. Standing between the two people he loved more than life, Matt smiled at them both. This was going to be a great night.

He opened the truck door, hoisting Davie up into the middle and buckling his seat belt. When Andie reached to hold his hand while she climbed inside, Matt's arm tingled with electric shock waves.

"Thank you," she murmured as she settled on the seat.

"You're welcome." He smiled, wondering at the

hammering of his heartbeat. He felt as giddy as a young kid out on his first date.

They shared a delicious meal together—rib-eye steak for Matt, roast chicken for Andie and a hamburger for Davie. With their son listening to every word, they weren't able to talk much about adult issues, and yet Matt thought that was best. He wanted them to be a family again. And that meant they needed to become comfortable friends first.

"To the most beautiful, accomplished wife a man could have." Matt leaned closer to Andie as he lifted his glass in a toast.

She hesitated, then reached for her glass. "To us."

Davie scurried to grasp his glass and ended up knocking it over. Both Matt and Andie simultaneously jerked back to keep from getting doused by milk.

A shocked expression covered Davie's face. Andie reached for her napkin and began to soak up the mess. Tears beaded in Davie's eyes, his little chin quivering. "I'm sorry."

Matt waved his hand to get the attention of a waiter. "No harm done, son. It'll clean up easily."

Matt couldn't help remembering a time when a mess like this might have upset him. Now he could think of a lot more serious issues he had to deal with. The last thing he wanted was to cry over spilled milk.

Instead, he reached over and hugged his son.

Andie kissed the boy's forehead. Davie smiled, sitting back and looking secure in his parents' love while the waiter sopped up the spill.

This was what Matt wanted more than anything else in the world. More than his career, fame or worldly possessions. Throughout their lives, they'd undoubtedly spill many glasses of milk. But as long as they forgave each other and clung to their family, they could face anything. Together.

They spent the rest of the evening laughing, eating hot mixed-berry cobbler with vanilla ice cream, and talking about summer activities. Davie grinned as he chewed, both cheeks bulging, a dollop of ice cream on his chin.

Because it was fire season, neither Matt nor Andie planned to take any summer vacations, but Matt hoped they might plan a skiing trip together for Christmas. There was plenty of time to broach the subject with her later.

Back at home, Matt carried a sleepy Davie inside the house where Andie stepped out of her high heels.

"They're sure pretty. Have you had enough of those torture devices?" Matt teased her.

She nodded with a smile. "Sometimes a woman's vanity causes her a lot of pain."

"Read me a bedtime story, Daddy." Davie rubbed his eyes and yawned.

"Okay, hotshot." Matt lifted the kid up on his

shoulder like an airplane and zoomed him around the room.

Davie squealed, now wide-awake.

Andie shook her head, one hand resting on her slim waist. "Matt, he was almost asleep. Don't get him wound up again."

Matt chuckled, but carried the boy to his room where he helped him put on his jammies and brush his teeth. When Davie knelt beside his small bed, bowed his head and folded his arms, Matt followed suit. He'd never prayed like this, but figured it was time.

Davie didn't ask for help, and Matt breathed a sigh of relief. As he listened to his son's simple request that God watch over his mommy and daddy, Matt felt abundant gratitude to Andie for teaching their son to love and depend upon the Lord.

"And please keep Mommy and Daddy safe when they fight wildfire."

A hard lump formed in Matt's throat.

Thank You, Lord. Thank You for giving me this wonderful little boy and his mother. And please forgive me for ever hurting them. Matt carried his own prayer silently in his heart.

"Now a story."

Andie listened outside Davie's bedroom door as he finished his prayer. Peeking around the doorjamb, she saw Davie hop into bed and Matt slowly stand.

After wrapping a light blanket over his son, Matt reached for a book and held it up for Davie's inspection. "This one?"

Davie shook his head and Matt tried again. "How about this one?"

"No, I want that one. It's my favorite." Davie pointed at a red book with Smokey the Bear on the front cover. A story about a child who played with matches and accidentally started a forest fire. Andie couldn't remember how many times she'd read the book to her boy. Maybe hundreds.

"Okay, hotshot, give me some room." Matt cuddled on the bed with his arms around his son and Davie leaning back against his chest.

Andie liked seeing them together like this. Her child deserved a loving father. Part of her was so happy to have Matt back in their lives. And yet, she felt more empty inside than ever before.

She wanted to forgive Matt. Just like that. She didn't want to be angry at him anymore. He'd suffered enough. So had she and Davie. But one thing still troubled her. Having witnessed firsthand how he'd frozen up during the fire training course, she knew they had to resolve this problem before they tackled another one. Matt needed psychological help. But how could she convince him of that?

As he read, Matt used voice inflection to act out the various parts of the story. A high tone for the little boy, a deep bass voice for Smokey Bear and a medium pitch for the forest ranger who came to the rescue and put out the fire. As he turned the page, he glanced her way and looked startled to find her there. He recovered quickly, giving her a wink and a smile.

Andie stood leaning against the doorjamb, her arms crossed as she listened. Now that he had an audience, Matt seemed to feel a bit embarrassed. He finished the story quickly, tickled his son one last time, kissed the boy on the forehead and headed for the door.

Andie disappeared, waiting in the hall. Before Matt flipped off the light, she heard Davie call to him.

"I love you, Daddy."

"I love you too, son."

Andie's heart squeezed hard. How could she continue to hold a grudge against this man? She couldn't. Not anymore. But she still wasn't sure that meant she was ready to trust him enough to let him move back into the house. That would take a giant leap of faith she wasn't yet certain she was ready to make.

Out in the living room, Andie sat in a soft chair, waiting for Matt to join her. No TV. No sounds but the crickets chirping outside the open window. A warm breeze teased the curtains, and she looked up. Matt stood in the doorway leading down the hall, watching her expectantly. What should she do? What should she say?

"Can we talk a few minutes before you leave?" she asked.

Okay, probably not what he wanted to hear on their marriage anniversary, but she'd met him half-way. She didn't want him to stay, but neither did she want him to go. Hopefully he could accept that.

He sat on the couch, leaning forward to rest his elbows on his knees and gaze into her eyes. "What did you want to talk about?"

"Nothing in particular. I had fun tonight. So did Davie. You're good with him. Can you believe he dug his church shirt out of the dirty clothes hamper so he could dress up tonight?"

He chuckled. "I noticed it was rumpled, but I didn't know it was dirty."

She nodded. "When I saw him with his hair slicked back like yours, I didn't have the heart to tell him to put on something different. It was obvious he wanted to look like you."

Matt's smile faded. "I never knew how much our kids learn from us. I wish I'd been around the past six years to show him a better example of how a good man should treat his family."

"I know, but you're here now. He'll soon forget you weren't there in his early years."

Could she forget? Could she really forgive and let it go?

He leaned back, resting his palms on the tops of his thighs. "I—I want to tell you something, but it won't be easy. I need to get it off my chest."

"Okay." She watched his face carefully as he began speaking, absorbing every word.

"You already know about the wildfire I was caught in. How it burned my legs. They didn't think I'd ever walk again. But I had to. So I could return to you." He closed his eyes, as if the memory was too much for him to bear.

"Matt, you don't need to tell me if you don't want to."

He opened his eyes. "But I do, Andie. I've got to tell someone I can trust. I'd followed all the rules, but we lost communication and we didn't know how bad the danger was. It was a small fire, only eighty acres. I thought we could hurry and finish up the fire line. Sixty-mile-per-hour winds whipped the fire to our flank, boxing us into the clearing."

He swallowed hard. "Jim and I...we deployed our fire shelters, but he had forgotten his gloves. I—I could hear him screaming. He couldn't withstand the pain and he—he bolted."

Matt paused, his voice hoarse and low. "Listening to someone die by fire isn't like in the movies. It took twenty minutes for Jim to die. I—I've never heard anything like it and hope I never hear those sounds again."

"Oh, Matt. I'm so sorry."

Tears streamed down his cheeks. "I couldn't stop it. I couldn't save Jim. I couldn't—"

He buried his face in his hands, choking with emotion. She reached out and wrapped her arms around him, holding him tight. It was the first time she'd shown him physical comfort since he'd returned.

He didn't pull away, his shoulders shaking. They both cried for several moments.

"Shh, it's okay now," she soothed, feeling helpless to console him.

Finally he lifted his head and wiped his reddened eyes. Seeing him so vulnerable made her feel protective of him.

"I don't know why I survived when Jim died. His wife and kids still need him. It should have been me who died, not him."

"Maybe Jim's family already knew their father loved them, and their memories would sustain them in the future. But Davie didn't know if his father loved him. Maybe God knew your son still needed you."

He looked deep into her eyes, as if her words had touched him like nothing else could. "Do you mean that, Andie?"

She nodded. "I do."

"And what about you? Do you still need me?" His voice broke and so did her heart.

She stared at their entwined fingers. Yes! She wanted to yell. *I need you, too.* So much. But it was too soon. Matt was carrying so much heavy baggage. She couldn't help worrying about his mental stability. "It's too soon for me to commit to anything right now, Matt. I do like having you around."

The confession came hard for her, but she realized it wasn't quite what he was after. It was all she could concede to right now. She didn't need him to live. She could provide for herself and Davie just fine. And yet, life seemed so hollow without Matt in it. Her heart continued to beat, but she had little joy, except for Davie. And she wanted more. Much, much more.

A shuddering breath escaped him. "Can you forgive me, Andie? Please?"

Her eyes met his. She saw the regret and sorrow he felt. The deep, abiding anguish tormenting his soul. So many vacant, empty words lay between them. Maybe God had spared Matt's life so they could have a second chance to say they were sorry. A second chance for Matt to be a daddy to Davie. Instead of always concentrating on past hurts, maybe she should focus on the potential good they could accomplish in their future together. Forgiving Matt didn't mean she wanted a marriage with him.

Or did she?

"I forgive you, if you'll forgive me." She said the words slowly, but didn't expect the instant feeling of relief that flooded her. Like a load of rocks had been lifted from her heart.

"I said a lot of hurtful, selfish things before you left. Things I didn't really mean. I was just scared, and I'm sorry." Tears flooded her eyes. It felt so good to apologize. She'd had no idea how bad she felt for her own part in their separation until she confessed it out loud.

A tender smile creased the corners of his mouth. "I guess we both messed up big time, huh?"

"Yes, we did."

He leaned near, until their noses touched. The subtle spicy scent of his cologne teased her nose. He kissed her gently, lovingly, and a sudden bolt of emotion surged through her. A gasp escaped her as she drew back and looked at him. She saw the passion in his eyes and realized he felt the same. After all this time, they still connected in a basic fundamental level of attraction. She wanted him, but she must move slowly. There was too much at stake.

"We still have a lot to sort out between us, Matt." She pressed her fingers to her lips, still feeling the warmth of his kiss there.

He blinked, looking uneasy. "Like what?"

"Like trust. What if you leave again? I don't want to be hurt like that once more. I have Davie to think about now."

He withdrew his hand from hers and turned away. For a fraction of a second, she almost reached out and pulled him back. Almost.

They'd made a lot of headway tonight. At least

they'd talked without her becoming so angry that she couldn't breathe. In fact, she felt quite calm right now. Matt had opened up to her for the first time, and in return, she'd been honest with him. They'd both apologized and forgiven each other, and it felt so good.

"Matt, I think we need a little more time before we…before we decide what to do about our marriage."

He shook his head, his features tense. "I don't need any more time, Andie. I know what I want. You and Davie. A real marriage with us living together in one house. You can trust me. I'll never leave you again. Even if you send me away, I'll keep coming back. I'm not going anywhere."

She heard the conviction in his voice and saw the truth written on his face. But what about the wildfire? What about the guilt haunting him?

What about love?

"You need to see a psychologist, Matt. You need to deal with your survivor's guilt and the horror of what happened to you."

He came to his feet so fast, the movement startled her. "I just told you about it. What more do you want from me?"

"Nothing. I just want you to be happy."

"I am happy here with you and Davie."

"But the wildfire is still there."

He released a small sigh. "It'll always be there,

Andie. It's part of who I am now. I have to live with it for the rest of my life."

"But it doesn't have to hurt you. That kind of darkness will canker inside of you. It'll cause more problems unless you deal with it now. What if you freeze up again?"

He raked a hand through his short hair. "I won't."

"You can't promise that, honey."

Honey. Now she'd stepped in it. If only she could help him see that he wasn't over the wildfire. It was still inside of him, like a dry keg of powder waiting for a lighted match.

His expression changed from anguish to bland. Gone was the emotion, replaced by the strong, in-control firefighter.

"Matt—"

"I'll think about it, okay? That's all I can say right now."

"Then that will have to be enough for now. But I'd feel better if it was what you wanted, too. You have to make yourself happy." How she wished she could heal his tattered soul. She wanted him whole again. More than anything else.

"I said I'd think about it." His voice hardened.

"Okay, that's better than nothing. But don't forget about the power of prayer. God is always there for us. We just need to ask Him for help. I've learned that the hard way after years of ignoring Him."

He stepped close and kissed her lightly on the

lips. "Thanks for a wonderful evening. I'll call you tomorrow."

He walked to the door, seeming eager to leave for the first time since his return. Obviously the conversation had become uncomfortable for him, and she didn't push it any further.

"Good night." He said the words mechanically, without enthusiasm.

And then he was gone.

Andie closed the door, watching out the window until his headlights disappeared before she turned off the porch light. Then she picked up her pretty high heels and went to her bedroom. In the quiet darkness, she exercised her own advice, kneeling beside her bed. She poured her heart out to God in a soft whisper. Asking Him to help Matt. Reaching for the faith she needed in order to trust her husband again with all her heart and confidence.

Reaching for peace.

Chapter Fourteen

When Matt didn't show up at church the next day, Andie worried. They'd forgiven each other, but the angst Matt still carried over the forest fire was a wild card. Anguish like that could plague a person without them even realizing it. She'd written a research paper in college about survivor's guilt and knew it could even make the survivor suicidal.

Was Matt depressed enough to take his own life? He seemed happy enough, until they brought up the topic of the wildfire. She wasn't a trained psychologist and couldn't diagnose him, but she was convinced he needed professional help.

"What's bothering you?" Brett asked as they walked out to the church parking lot.

Her gaze flickered to Sue and the baby, walking ahead with Davie. "I'll give you one guess."

Brett nodded, his hair slicked back as he carried his scriptures and the diaper bag. "Matt. It's hard to be angry with someone you love."

She stared at him with denial, then softened. "Does it show that much?"

"Afraid so. Why fight it?"

"You know why. Just because you love someone doesn't mean you're willing to become their doormat. You can forgive someone and still not be with them."

"Do you want to be with Matt again?"

"No!" she answered too fast, then amended. "Well, yes and no. He's so full of hurt over the wildfire, Brett. I really don't know how stable he is right now. I saw the wild look in his eyes and it frightened me. What if he lost control of himself or decided to leave again?"

He shrugged, looking nice in his pin-striped suit. "He's served like a rock through a lot of fires, Andie. He's been stable in his career, until he lost a man. But I think deep inside what's really bothering him is that he left you. Maybe he equates losing his crewman with losing you. And that scares him more than he realizes."

Her heels tapped the concrete as she stepped off the sidewalk into the parking lot. Reaching into her purse, she pulled out her car keys and remembered when Matt had watched Davie for her while she worked on the small brush fire. He'd looked so relieved when she'd returned. She'd realized he'd worried about her, but maybe it was more than that.

"He told me the combination of losing his crewman and almost dying in the wildfire made him reevaluate his priorities," she said.

"That's understandable. And the wildfire can be a blessing, if you look at it that way. Sometimes it only takes a little drama to get our attention. But other times, the Lord has to really hit us hard to wake us up to what's really important in life. You and Matt have been given a second chance at happiness, Andie. I hope you both can work it out."

"Brett, will you open the car, please?" Sue called to her husband. She stood beside their blue sedan, looking frustrated as she balanced Rose and waited to get the baby in her car seat.

"Sure, honey. See you later, Andie." Brett hurried to help his wife, leaving Andie alone with her thoughts.

Had God saved Matt's life so they could have a second chance together? So they could be a family? She trusted the Lord and knew He only did what was best for His children. Maybe she should listen to the spirit more. She might learn something.

As soon as she and Davie got home from church, she called Matt, just to make sure he was okay.

"Hi, Andie. What's up?" He'd obviously seen her name on caller ID.

"Hi! We missed you in church. You doing okay?"

"Yeah, I've just got a lot on my mind and needed some time to think."

"Is there anything I can do?"

"No, I'm fine." He answered fast. Too fast. She

couldn't help wondering if he was just telling her what he thought she wanted to hear, or if it was the truth.

She held the phone receiver closer to her ear. "What are you thinking so hard about?"

"You really want to know?"

"Yes." Her answer came out slow and guarded, but truthfully.

"I'm thinking about you and me and how I can be the kind of man you deserve. I let you down, sweetheart, and I never want to do that again."

Well, she'd asked, so she deserved the answer she got. "You wouldn't do anything to hurt yourself, would you, Matt? I mean, that would just tear Davie and me apart. It'd only make things worse."

He snorted. "Stop worrying. I'm definitely not suicidal. I want to live. I want to be happy."

She wanted to believe him, but couldn't help fretting. "You want to come over for dinner? I'm fixing your favorite. Lasagna and French bread."

"Hmm. Lots of delicious calories. You're the best cook I know."

"So come over." She couldn't believe she was actually pushing for him to come see her, but she didn't want him to be alone. Deep inside, she sensed they'd made gigantic headway in working through his anguish, and he had to be feeling vulnerable right now. In spite of her vow to never let him into her life again, she wanted to help. To be close to him once more.

A long pause followed. "Not today. I'm wrestling with what we talked about last night. Just give me some time, okay? I promise I'll make everything up to you in the end."

Now she was even more worried. How stable was her husband? She may have pushed him too hard.

"Matt, you promised you wouldn't leave us again, and I'm holding you to it."

His voice lowered. "Thanks, I needed to hear that. Now don't worry."

"But I am worried." Maybe she was confiding too much of how she felt. What did it matter? She was crazy about him. She always had been. She didn't want to pretend anymore. What use was it to deny her feelings? And yet, there was a dark part of him she didn't recognize. A part that scared her.

"Well don't. Everything's gonna be okay. I'll talk to you tomorrow."

"Okay, tomorrow."

"Bye."

She hung up after he did. Wishing she could be there for him the way he'd been there for her lately.

She went about her routine, fixing Davie a quiet dinner at home. As an excuse to check up on her husband, she had Davie call Matt two more times. She wanted to remind Matt that he had a son who would be devastated if anything happened to his father. Each time Matt answered, he laughed and chatted like normal. Maybe she was worried about nothing.

No, an inner wisdom warned her it wasn't that easy. Matt needed help. She felt powerless and alone. And that's when she turned to the Lord in prayer.

Just after Davie went to sleep for the night, she knelt beside her bed and poured her heart out to God. She told Him everything that had been locked away inside of her the past six years. All the anger, hurt and hatred came rushing out. She cried and gnashed her teeth. She let it go.

And then came hope. And love. A desire to reconcile with her husband and restore her family once more. The expectations she didn't dare express to anyone but God. When she finished, she felt exhausted and mentally drained. Glancing at the clock, she saw that two hours had passed. She needed to sleep.

As she climbed into bed, she formulated a plan of action. Tomorrow, she would go to Matt's office and ask to take him to lunch. Irrespective of whether they got back together, she loved and worried about him. He'd left her, but he'd come home. She wouldn't abandon him, no matter what. He needed help and she would see that he got it, before it was too late.

* * *

Andie didn't get the chance to activate her plan. A lightning storm kept her awake most of the night, and she figured they'd have a wildfire soon.

The next morning, she dropped Davie off at Sue's house and arrived at her office before eight. The air felt hot and muggy. The damp pavement and pungent smell of rain caused her to gaze at the mountains. Rainstorms in June meant fire was just a matter of time.

Inside the ranger station, she walked by her receptionist's desk. Clarice waved a pink paper and chimed in a cheerful voice, "Morning, Andie. The Forest Supervisor's office just called and asked if you could go over there to meet with Cal Hinkle first thing."

Andie paused and leaned against the high counter, gazing at the paper in her hand. Cal's name and phone number were written at the top. "Did his assistant say what it was about?"

"Nope, just that it was urgent that he speak with you in person."

Andie nodded and headed for her office, calling over her shoulder. "Call them back and tell them I'll be there in twenty minutes."

Clarice nodded and picked up the phone.

Wondering what the emergency was, Andie drove to the S.O.'s office. After entering the redbrick building, she checked in with the front receptionist.

"Go right in. He's expecting you," the woman said.

Andie turned, then paused. "And can you tell me if Matt Cutter's in today?"

The receptionist nodded. "He's always the first one here in the mornings, but I think he's meeting with someone right now."

Andie breathed a sigh of relief as she walked down the hall to Cal's office. When she passed by Matt's office, she peeked at the nameplate on his door. The door was closed, but she could see a stream of light shining beneath. At least he was here, safe and sound.

Thinking no more about it, she continued down the hall where Cal's admin assistant immediately led her into his office.

"Andie! Thanks for coming in on such short notice." Cal stood and rounded his spacious desk. He shook her hand before closing the door. "Have a seat."

She sat in one of the leather chairs facing his desk and crossed her legs. Feeling self-conscious, she ran a hand down the pant leg of her crisp ranger's uniform, trying not to feel nervous. "What's up?"

His chair creaked as he sat down. "Let me get right to the point. I've heard that you and Matt Cutter are married."

Oh, no! Was he angry with her? A blaze of dread shivered up her spine. "Yes, but…"

"And I understand you're separated." A statement, not a question.

She nodded, unwilling to trust her voice right now. Surely he'd spoken to Matt about this issue since his office was just down the hall. Yet Matt hadn't mentioned anything to her about it.

"And you have a little boy," Cal continued.

"Y...yes, Davie."

Cal smiled. "I've seen pictures of him in Matt's office. A cute kid. And from what Matt's told me, he's a natural athlete."

"He is. A wonderful boy."

And? What did Cal want? Her mind raced with urgency.

"I didn't know you and Matt were married and separated when I hired both of you to work on this national forest. Otherwise, I wouldn't have done so."

"I didn't know he was taking the job, either, until I'd already moved to Enlo and started working here. I've been going by my maiden name since Matt...since Matt and I separated. I think this was just a fluke."

He nodded, not looking flustered in the least. "It's a rarity, but it happens sometimes. I want to offer you a transfer to Evanston, Wyoming."

Andie's heart dropped to her toes. A transfer? That would mean packing up Davie and leaving Nevada. Because she and Matt happened to be married. She could just imagine what that would do to her son. Regaining his father only to lose him again. And what about her? She looked forward to Matt's visits to her house. He'd brought a sense of security and happiness into her life, and she didn't want to lose that ever again.

"But I just got settled here."

"I know, but I sensed some difficulty between you and Matt several months ago, and now I understand why. I think you'll remember that I asked you about it." He lifted his brows in a stern look.

"Yes, but we've done fine working together. Our relationship isn't a problem for us, Cal. Really. I've nosedived into the work and my marriage hasn't impacted it in anyway."

She couldn't leave Nevada. Not now. Not when she and Matt were finally reconciling. Not when they'd finally forgiven each other.

Cal sat back and placed his hands on the armrests of his chair. "I've been extremely happy with both your and Matt's work performance. In fact, I hate to lose either one of you. You're an asset to this forest. But I don't want you to feel uncomfortable working with Matt so that it starts to impact your work."

"It won't. Matt and I have talked about this. We're professionals. We know what to do."

He chuckled. "You don't need to convince me, Andie. And you don't have to take the transfer, either."

"We don't…er, I don't? Really?" She shook her head, putting every ounce of seriousness into her expression.

"No. Do you want to stay here in Enlo?"

"Yes." A quick, sharp nod.

Cal pursed his lips together. "It's funny, but Matt said the same thing."

She curled her hands together in her lap. She didn't move. Didn't breathe. "You asked Matt if he wanted a transfer?"

"Yeah, several weeks ago. An FCO position in Oregon has opened up, and they requested Matt by name. It'd mean a promotion for him. Since he's rehabilitated and doing so well, I offered him the job."

She tensed. "And is he going to take it?"

"No. He said he'd quit the forest service before he left his family again. When I asked where he'd work, he said it didn't matter as long as he could be near you and Davie. Knowing you two are separated, I figured he still cares a lot for his family."

Andie's mouth dropped open. "He actually said those things?"

"Much more graphically, but yes. He said nothing was more important than being near his family. He won't go anywhere without you."

An overwhelming joy enveloped Andie. So powerful that she almost wept with it. "I agree. I won't let my family be separated again. If it's all the same to you, I'd prefer staying right where I am. I'm happy. Truly happy here."

Cal threw back his head and laughed. "Okay, then. It's settled. The Cutter family is gonna stay right here in Enlo. I hope this means a reconciliation might be forthcoming. Matt's been through a lot, and I'd love nothing more than to see you two back together."

She smiled, but didn't reply. She liked this idea more and more. A reconciliation. The Cutter family. It had a nice ring to it. Now if she could just work things out with Matt.

When she returned to her ranger station, Andie stepped inside just as a fierce gust of wind whipped the door away from her hand. The door slammed closed with a loud bang and she flinched, grateful the glass panes didn't break. She brushed hair out of her eyes, thinking such a wind would be disastrous for a wildfire.

Urgency caused her to hurry to her office. She planned to call Matt and schedule a meeting at her place later that evening. She'd see if Sue could watch Davie for her, and then Andie would fix dinner for Matt. They needed time alone. He'd been offered a promotion…and he'd turned it down. So he could stay with his family. Matt had changed after all.

The fire dispatch interrupted her thoughts, tapping against her door as he leaned through the threshold. "Andie, we've got a fire. A resident living in Lee was out hiking and spotted smoke."

She blinked, transitioning her mind back to business. "Where?"

"Near Harrison Pass. It's on BLM land, spreading fast. We've got a campground nearby."

With these winds, the fire could spread fast. Numerous ranches dotted the valleys surrounding the Ruby Mountains along with cabins, mines and personal property. It all needed protection.

"We could have a number of small spot fires, too," Andie said.

"Yeah, we could."

"Okay, I'll come down to your office for a more detailed report in just a minute."

With a nod, he disappeared and Andie reached for her phone. Her personal desire to talk to Matt would have to wait. Knowing this routine well, she first called Susan. Davie was always her main priority, and she wanted to ensure he'd be taken care of while she was busy with the fire.

"Hello." Sue's voice sounded cheerful.

"Hi, sis. I just wanted to inform you that we've got a fire burning on BLM land that's spreading rapidly. I may need you to watch Davie overnight for me."

"Of course. Where's the fire?" Sue asked.

Andie explained the location.

"Is it a big fire?"

"Getting that way. I was just outside and the

wind is horrible, so I'm expecting it to take a while to get things under control."

"Whatever you need. Just take care of yourself."

Andie scrunched her shoulder up to hold the phone to her ear. With her hands free, she reached for her fire pack sitting on the floor behind her office door. During fire season, she kept it packed and ready at a moment's notice. "Will do. I'll call you periodically to check on Davie and give you updates on when I'll be home. Tell him I love him."

"Of course I will. Is Matt involved?"

Andie hesitated, not wanting to get into an ugly discussion with her sister right now. She'd squared Sue on her treatment of Matt, but sensed her sister still didn't like him much. "I'm planning to call him next. As the fire control officer, he needs to be aware of every fire impacting the forest. You know that."

"Yeah, I know that."

Andie released a sigh. "Look, Sue. Matt's been spending more and more time at my house. We went out to dinner for our anniversary, and he told me about the wildfire he was injured on. We— we've forgiven each other."

Sue made an ugly sound. "What did you do that requires his forgiveness?"

"I said some pretty ugly things and sent him away. I'm just as much to blame as he is."

"You didn't hog-tie him and force him to go. We all have disagreements in our marriage, but that doesn't mean our men are gonna take off because of it."

Andie took a deep breath. "Sue, I say this with love and compassion. It's not your business. It's mine. And I just want to forget and move on with our lives."

"That's good, I suppose." Sue's voice sounded hesitant.

"You suppose?"

"Well, if you can forgive me for deleting Matt's phone calls, I suppose I shouldn't hold a grudge against him for deserting you. He really told you about the wildfire he was injured on?"

Andie's heart beat faster just thinking about what Matt had gone through. "Yeah, he's hurting inside, with good reason. I want to help him."

"You're not falling for him again out of sympathy, are you?"

Andie gripped the phone hard. "Not out of sympathy, but I think he's suffered enough, don't you?"

Sue coughed. "I suppose."

"He's still my husband, sis. You may need to adjust to the idea of us getting back together again."

"Do you love him?"

"I never stopped." Saying the words out loud seemed to take away Andie's fear. She loved him. She wanted to be with him. Forever.

"And does Matt love you?"

"He's made it clear he wants to be with Davie and me."

A pregnant pause followed. "But has Matt said the words to you?"

Andie took a long time in responding, her voice whisper soft. "Not exactly, but I haven't been too receptive until now."

Sue asked another question. "You don't think it's too soon to get back together?"

Andie released a deep breath. "I think we've been apart long enough."

Sue gave a half-hearted laugh. "Yeah, you have. If you love each other, then it's time. But don't worry about me. I'll be nice to him and support you in whatever you decide. No matter what, we'll always be sisters."

A feeling of relief warmed Andie's heart. She adored her sister and didn't want her marriage to come between them. "Amen to that. Thanks, Sue. I appreciate it. And I love you. Now I've got to go."

"I love you, too. Talk to you later."

Andie hung up the phone, a strange feeling of elation pulsing through her veins. *If she and Matt got back together.* She could actually imagine her fondest wish becoming a reality. She'd forgiven Matt. Really forgiven him. And he'd forgiven her. In place of the anger and hate, she felt peace and love. A lightness of heart she hadn't felt in years. As if they could forget the past and start over fresh. Like they could be great together and a real family again.

But did Matt love her? He'd told her he never

should have left her. That he wanted to be a family again. But he hadn't said the word *love*. Which made her wonder if his regret was inspired by guilt.

She shook her head. "You're overthinking this, Andie. Just focus on the fire, and you can talk with Matt about this later."

Rather than have the dispatcher call Matt's office, Andie dialed the number herself. As she did so, the truth nagged at her. What if he didn't love her? What if he just felt guilty for leaving her? She had no doubt he loved Davie. But loving a child and loving his mother were two different things. Before she got back together with Matt, she had to know the truth. They still had a lot to talk about.

"Minden National Forest. Sherry speaking."

"Hi, Sherry. It's Andie Cutter, er, Foster. Is Matt available?"

"I'm sorry, Andie, but he's in a meeting. Can I take a message and have him return your call?"

Andie sighed. She longed to hear Matt's voice. She'd been so happy, confessing her love for him. Uncertain whether he felt the same about her.

She'd just have to wait. In a few concise sentences, she relayed the fire information to Sherry, then headed down to her dispatcher's office. Within thirty minutes, she was dressed in her yellow fire-resistant shirt, white helmet and Nomex pants. She gazed out the windshield, concentrating on the road as she and her range assistant drove west on Interstate 228 toward the Ruby Mountains. An engine and fire crew accompanied her: twenty men and women composed of a resource crew boss, a squad boss, an advanced firefighter, and sixteen less-advanced firefighters. They were ready for battle.

Her talk with Matt would have to wait.

Chapter Fifteen

Andie leaned her hip against the map table her crew had set up at base camp beneath a large open-air tent. Hand crews of firefighters, engines fully loaded with retardant foam, large cats with plows attached, water tenders holding fifteen-hundred gallons of water, dozers and pumper trucks all moved across the area like a well-oiled machine.

The staging area rested at the base of the Ruby Mountains, just outside of Lee, Nevada. Catering stands with eating tables, portable toilets and showers, tents for sleeping, and telephones had been brought in, turning the base camp into a small community of three thousand men and women overnight.

The command team stood around the table, all of them gazing at the map. As the operations chief, Matt led the discussion. He leaned over the map and pointed at key areas, his strong fingers a bit dirty from working. "What we've got here is a

Class D fire, covering over five thousand acres. We're fighting the main fire out of Harrison Pass. We've also got hand crews working to flank and pinch out a number of spot fires."

"Where are our spot fires?" Hank Dittmer, the incident commander, asked.

"Here by Ruby Dome, Griswold Lake, Verdi Peak and Echo Canyon."

"Echo Canyon? Don't we have a crew working just below Echo Lake?" Andie asked.

Matt straightened, his gaze meeting hers. "Yes, a type-one crew. They should have six programmable radios, but I'm concerned. We lost communication with them over an hour ago. They haven't checked in."

"That terrain is rugged and inaccessible. Why'd we send a crew up there?" Hank asked.

Andie had heard this before. *Rugged and inaccessible* had become a justification for inaction. "It's inaccessible for pumpers, but a crew can handle it as long as they can work safely. If we ignore this fire, it'll just get bigger and we'll lose the opportunity to take control. They learned that with the South Canyon fire back in 1994."

Matt frowned. "That's right, but now Echo Canyon is acting like a chimney and we've got a buttonhook fire creeping over from below."

Andie nodded in agreement. "I doubt the fire crew is aware of the danger. That canyon is filled with flash fuels, high temperatures, low humidity and squirrely winds going in and out. It's a tragedy waiting to happen."

Hank Dittmer pressed his palms against the tabletop as he perused the map. "We need to send a chopper in right now to see if we can find and warn the crew of the danger."

"We certainly do," Andie agreed.

"I'll do it," Matt offered.

Everyone looked at him, no one seeming to think his proposal odd, except for Andie. "Matt, you can't go in. You don't know the area."

"Yes, I do. I hiked a number of the canyons on Ruby Mountain while I was training for my work-capacity test. Echo Canyon was one of them, although it took me two days to hike up to Echo Lake. It was rough going, but if I hike in from above, I should be able to reach the crew within an hour."

Andie stared at him, her mouth hanging open. So much for trying to claim he didn't know the area and couldn't go in. "You did?"

"Yep. I'll take the small spotter chopper and see if I can find the crew." Matt picked up his binoculars and peered through them as he scanned the mountain, training his gaze south toward Ruby Dome—the vicinity where the fire crew was working.

Without looking, Andie knew a cloud of black smoke billowed across the mountain with red flames licking beneath. Spot fires dotted the mountains, running downhill toward the numerous ranches sprinkled across the valley below. They'd called in hotshot crews from states across the nation and firefighters from almost every agency in Nevada to help. This was a big fire, and they had yet to gain control.

"That sounds like a good plan. Let me know as soon as the crew is evacuated from the area," Hank said.

Matt lowered the binoculars and glanced at his watch. "It's noon and already the air is hot."

Hank nodded. "Yes, and the winds are escalating the fire. I've called in smoke jumpers to help the hotshot crews."

Matt set the binoculars aside. "My past experience tells me the temperatures will climb high enough by midafternoon that the fire could explode up the canyon. The hotshot crew is working at the top of a chimney. If it explodes—"

Andie listened to this conversation with dread. On the one hand, Matt seemed calm and collected. The experienced wildfire fighter who knew his business. But what if he got up on the mountain and froze up? Once the chopper dropped him off, he'd need to hike across rocky terrain to the fire crew. He'd be all alone. No one to help him. If he panicked or lost control, he could become disoriented and die.

On the other hand, if she objected strongly enough, it might come out that Matt had frozen up during a simple training operation and wasn't of sound mind. Not only would that embarrass him, but it could also destroy his career, not to mention any reconciliation with Andie. It'd devastate him and he'd hate her. She couldn't do that to him. Yet she couldn't let him endanger his life, either.

She didn't want him to go.

"When can you leave?" Hank asked.

"As soon as I get to the helipad," Matt said.

No! This was moving way too fast.

"Matt, can I speak with you privately for a few moments?" Andie's voice wobbled.

"Sure." He rounded the table and followed her a short distance away where they could speak without someone listening in.

She took a breath and started to cough, the smoke-filled air burning her eyes. She rubbed them, hoping to ease the gritty feeling.

"What's up?" he asked.

She faced him, meeting his gaze. He looked so handsome in his fire uniform. Handsome and strong. "Matt, don't do this. You're not ready to go."

He smiled. "Sure I am. I've been training and preparing for this all my life."

"But what about the wildfire when you were injured? I know that scarred you on the inside as well as on the outside. You haven't dealt with it yet."

He licked his lips and rested his hands on his

lean hips. "I've been dealing with it in my own way. You'll be happy to know I saw a psychologist."

"You did?" Could she believe him?

"Yes, and I confided what happened on the wild-fire. You were right. It felt good to talk about it and get it off my chest. I know I have a purpose in life. It's not my time to go yet."

She peered at him, feeling skeptical. "How many times have you seen this doctor?"

"Once, yesterday morning. I have another appointment next week. But it's the Lord who's really given me the therapy I need, Andie. I can't explain it, but He's been there for me like my best friend. I know He loves me. He's watching out for us always."

She snorted, lifting a hand to brush a wisp of hair out of her eyes. "One visit to the doctor isn't going to make you whole again. You need time. It'll take a lot of work."

"That's just it, Andie. I've been working on this problem for months now. And I don't want it to ruin my life."

"Then don't go up on that mountain."

"Now isn't the time for this, Andie. But the point is that I've talked about what happened. To you and to my doctor. It hasn't been easy, but I feel better already. And I finally understand why God spared my life."

"You do?"

"Yes. So I could come home to you. To tell you

how sorry I am and to be a father to Davie. It's so clear to me now. And I'm awed by the Lord's kindness. I regret that Jim died, but I made a promise to myself that I'd honor his memory by being the best man I possibly can. So he wouldn't have died in vain."

The conviction in his voice touched her like nothing else could. "I'm glad to hear you say that. I'm so glad you've developed a close relationship with God."

"Then you'll understand why I'm going up to Echo Lake."

She flinched. "Please don't."

"I'll be okay, hon." He squeezed her hand.

When he turned his back and headed toward the command tent, he didn't limp at all. She almost burst into tears. But she couldn't. She was the ranger and must be an example to the people around her. She must remain strong and focused.

Matt picked up his fire pack and slung it over his shoulder as though the heavy weight was light as a daisy. She stared at him from head to toe, the fire-resistant shirt and wildfire boots with heavy lug soles and nine-inch tops extending up his calves.

She followed him, not ready to give in. "Matt—"

He spoke low so other people wouldn't hear him. "I can't hide just because I was hurt, Andie. They say when you get bucked off, you get right back on and ride again."

"You were more than bucked off, Matt. One of

your men died in that fire. I saw how you reacted during the training exercise. Someone else can go up to Echo Lake. Even me."

"No, absolutely not. You're not going." He shook his head, his bloodshot eyes narrowed with determination. As part of the command team, they'd been living on four hours of sleep for the past three days.

"Why not? I'm not as experienced as you are, but I have the training."

He reached out and brushed his knuckles against her cheek, looking deep into her eyes. "I know, sweetheart, but Davie needs you. Thank you for worrying about me, but I'm gonna be okay. Have a little faith."

"No. Let's wait another hour and see if we hear from the crew. Maybe they're just busy and not paying attention."

He shook his head, his stubborn jaw locked hard. "By then, it could be too late. If they don't have an escape route, they'll need time to clear an area. I'm going in to warn them now, before we lose any lives. I won't lose another man on my watch. Not if I can help it."

"Matt, please—"

"I'm happy, Andie. For the first time in a long time, I feel at peace. It hasn't been easy, but the Lord's helped me realize that I can choose to be happy in my life regardless of what happens to me. I've chosen to be happy."

What was he talking about? "What does that have to do with fighting wildfire?"

"I'm not afraid anymore, babe. I've turned my life over to the Lord. I can accept whatever He plans for me. Besides, I outrank you."

A sick feeling washed over her. "You wouldn't pull rank on me."

"Try me." He tilted his head, a lopsided grin curving his mouth.

She didn't see anything humorous about the situation. "That's really low."

"Sorry, but I'm going in. Now do your job and pray that I reach them in time."

He turned to walk toward a green Forest Service truck. She knew he'd drive to the helipad they'd set up half a mile away and fly up on the mountain where he'd be dropped off at a remote site and hike down to the hotshot crew.

She clasped his arm and pulled him back, glancing around to see who might be watching their exchange. In the sea of fire personnel, equipment and smoke, it seemed she and Matt were all alone. An island unto themselves. "Is that what this is all about? You feel you need to prove yourself by rescuing that crew?"

He shook his head. "No, I don't need to prove myself. But someone needs to go in, Andie. And I'm the operations chief. It's my job to ensure the safety of my people above all else."

She stared at the bright red neck shroud he wore

around his throat. During heavy fire, he could pull it up to protect his face and lungs. "Where are your goggles?"

"Right here." He patted one of the deep cargo pockets on his Nomex pants.

This couldn't be happening. "You'll be all alone up there. If you get into trouble, there won't be anyone to help you."

Her voice rose to a shrill whisper. Panic dotted her skin. She couldn't let him go. She couldn't lose him. Not again.

He brushed his fingertips against her lips, soft and loving. "I won't be alone, Andie. The Lord will be with me, and so will you."

If only she could have as much faith as he did. "Matt, please—"

He kissed her, soft yet urgent. She gripped folds of his shirt with her hands, not wanting to let him go.

"I love you. So much. I'll be back." He spoke against her hair.

I love you. The magic words she'd longed to hear.

She didn't think to react until he'd pulled away. Her head spun dizzily, and she couldn't digest what was happening. Then he was gone. She went still, her breath coming in shallow gasps. She barely had time to gather her wits before he climbed inside the truck, started the engine and drove away.

He looked back at her in his rearview mirror.

She jogged after him, wanting to stop him somehow. Did he have a death wish? Just how stable was he? Maybe she was worried about nothing. And yet, she couldn't take the chance. Not when it might mean his life.

She glanced at another truck, tempted to chase after him. But she couldn't. She was needed here at the command station. She couldn't leave her post. And she couldn't stop him, either.

If only Matt hadn't passed the arduous level of his work-capacity test, he wouldn't be able to go. But he had. She had no right to question his authority. No right to worry about him now. He was a trained professional, and she had to let him go.

She pressed a hand to her mouth, biting down on her index finger. Any number of things could go wrong.

"Hey, Andie, you okay? You look white as a ghost." Phil, her fire assistant, entered the open-air tent, staring at her face.

"I'm fine." She looked away so he wouldn't see the alarm in her eyes. Or the tears. Forest rangers didn't cry. Not about this. And yet, she had so much to lose. Just when she and Matt had found each other again, he might be taken away. She and Davie loved and needed Matt so much.

Davie! What would she tell her son if something bad happened to his father?

Please, Lord. Please watch over Matt. Keep him safe and bring him home to me.

The prayer filled her heart. Never had she prayed so hard in all her life. All she could rely on now was her faith in God.

Another man came inside the tent and Andie recognized him as Alex Merritt, the branch director working underneath Matt. "You know we've got a hotshot crew working up above that buttonhook fire. We need to reestablish communication with them."

Phil jerked his thumb toward Andie. "The forest ranger's husband just flew in to locate and warn them."

Andie flinched, staring at Phil in surprise. The forest ranger's husband. Her husband.

Alex smiled at her. "You're Mrs. Cutter?"

She nodded, unwilling to trust her voice right now.

"Well, Matt's the best man we have for the job. If anyone knows how to hike in during an emergency like this, it's Matt."

There was no denying the tone of trust in Alex's voice. Andie picked up her binoculars and stared at the mountain. Thick smoke the color of gray slate hovered above the canyon. Beneath the haze, red flames flickered upward, eating at the fuel. Superheated flash fuels surrounded the steep slopes, fanned by erratic winds. An extremely volatile situation. And that was where her husband was going.

Into the fire.

And then Andie realized something she hadn't

thought of before. This was what Matt did. What he was good at. Because of his training and experience, he was a valuable national resource. She had hated his career with a vengeance. Hated it because it had taken him away from her. She hadn't realized how much he loved his job. How good he was at it. How much the Forest Service needed qualified men like him to save other people's lives and property.

She'd been selfish, loving a man, yet not wanting to let him be who he had to be. But no matter what, she wanted him back. For good this time. She loved him with every fiber of her being, and she might never get the chance to tell him how she felt.

Andie went through the motions of working at the command station, but her insides felt like jelly. She felt completely helpless and alone. All she had was prayer and faith to get her through. She carried both silently within her heart. Watching and waiting for her husband to come home safe.

Chapter Sixteen

Matt trained his binoculars on the fire crew working below him. Sitting in the small spotter chopper high above, he scanned the rocky crevices of the mountain below and felt a sense of relief. He'd found them. Now he had to get down to them and help them evacuate as quickly as possible.

The whir of the chopper blades overhead brought their attention, and they looked up from their work. One of the men waved, looking like a small stick figure from Matt's vantage point. If only the man knew the danger he was in, he'd be running for his life.

Thick streams of smoke wafted toward the east. The chopper circled around, staying back far enough that it didn't become engulfed by the smoke and lose visibility. From this angle, the fire seemed harmless. But Matt knew up close, it was an inferno, the temperatures more than five hundred degrees. Hot enough to melt flesh, scorch lungs, and kill a man before the flames even touched him. And the hotshot crew of men and women were working down there, not even realizing what they would soon be facing.

"Eight, nine, ten…" Matt counted off the twenty-man crew, then scanned the area for the helicopter to land. Verdi Peak was too far away, and it'd take him too long to hike in to the crew. They needed another place.

"What about that higher, flat area over there?" The pilot pointed above the ridge where the crew was working.

Two bighorn sheep ran west across the open area, fleeing the fire. On any other day, Matt would have scrambled for his camera.

The landing place wasn't far from the fire crew. From the looks of the steep cliffs and loose boulders, Matt knew the hike down into the canyon would be difficult. "It looks like the closest spot. Set her down."

The pilot steered the small spotter plane, capable of carrying just four people at a time. They'd come full circle and now flew above the smoke, which was so thick they couldn't see the ground below. Farther out, Matt could see the blackened ruins of what had already been consumed by the flames. Smoke streamed from numerous spot fires across the mountain—like steam from a teapot. A fierce gust of wind buffeted the plane, and Matt slammed back against his seat.

"Whoa! Glad we've got our seat belts on," the pilot said.

The chopper bumped down on the flat rocks, and the pilot held it still while Matt picked up his gear and got out.

"I'll fly back to command and refuel, then return by the time you've got the crew here to fly them out," the pilot said.

"Okay." Matt reached for his radio as the chopper lifted off in a whir of wind and dust.

"Cutter to Olston. Come in." Matt pressed the button on his radio, calling in his safe landing to command first thing.

A brief pause of static followed.

"This is Olston, go ahead."

"I'm on the ground west of Verdi Peak. Heading down to Echo Lake now. Copy?"

"Affirmative. Let us know when you reach the crew."

"Will do. Over."

Matt stowed his radio and waved at the pilot, then turned his gaze down the mountain. He knew exactly where he was. The chopper would return in about an hour, with the hope of ferrying the hotshot crew to safety just as soon as Matt could move them to the landing site.

Matt started out at a fast walk, but paced himself so he didn't tire prematurely. Every fifteen minutes, he reached for his canteen, taking a long drink without breaking stride. In this heat, he needed to remain hydrated. It could mean the difference between collapsing and survival.

As he passed Echo Lake, he could imagine the Mackinaw Lake trout just waiting for a fishing line. Maybe he'd bring Andie and Davie up here to camp out sometime. Although he'd rather come from the opposite direction, riding horses up the canyon.

Thinking about Andie caused him to focus his attention on the task at hand. He'd talked big for her benefit, to reassure her and help her not to worry. But as thin streams of smoke billowed past him, he started to doubt his own faith. He must be crazy to be up on this mountain. What if the winds changed on him? What if he couldn't get the crew out in time?

No! People were depending on him, and he mustn't let them down. To fail might mean death, for them and for him.

Instead of worrying, he prayed. Silently in his heart, asking God to be with him. To help him stay strong, no matter what he faced. Talking to his Father in Heaven helped him be spiritually strong, and he grasped a heavy stick to help him walk across the sharp rocks.

He skirted thick clusters of dwarf willow bushes, thinking it'd take less time to go around than to try to hack through the dense brush. They also might be filled with snakes and hornets.

The steep cliffs high above the lake forced him

to weave past loose boulders. The sharp rocks of the canyon rolled beneath his feet, but he could make quicker headway traveling down to the fire crew than hiking up.

Looking up, he saw a mountain goat hurrying past the razor-sharp ridge. Even the animals had enough sense to flee, but not him. He kept going, scrambling across the steep scree fields. He lost his balance and slid on his stomach several feet before regaining his hold. A *whoosh* escaped him as the air was knocked from his lungs. His body scraped against the prickly rocks. Thank goodness he wore his Nomex gloves to protect his hands from being sliced up.

He lay there, panting heavily to catch his breath. "Now I know why nothing but bighorn sheep and mountain goats live up here. Nothing else can negotiate the rugged terrain."

He turned his head and blinked. Right in front of his face, a delicate yellow primrose sat tucked back between the rocks. Reaching out, he picked the flower and sat up, tucking the blossom inside his shirt pocket. He'd give it to Andie when he saw her again.

He wiped his sweaty brow, determined to forge on. Instead of climbing back up the cliff, he stood and skirted the edge. A hard fall could break his legs or worse. He must be careful. Too many people's lives depended on his success.

After a half hour of strenuous hiking, the smoke

became thicker and he felt the heat like a blasting furnace to his face. Staying away from narrow draws and chutes, he followed the trailhead and passed a high, rocky ridge. The sound of chain saws breaking up fuel filled his ears. The fire crew was working just below him. He breathed a deep sigh of relief.

"Hello!" Matt waved and yelled.

One of the crewmen looked up and waved back. Except for Andie, Matt had never been so happy to see someone in his life.

Now that his goal was in sight, he hurried down. His first objective was to create an escape route for the crew. One by one, he passed each crew member working along the fire line. In a few succinct sentences, he gave them instructions.

"How many in your squad?" he asked the first man he met.

"Nine."

"Start moving your crew up the mountain now." He pointed to where the chopper would pick them up.

"What's the deal?"

"We'll talk about it later. Just comply." He sent each person on their way, expecting immediate obedience. This was a highly trained hotshot crew, and they should know better than to question his authority.

"Will do." Each man and woman stowed their tools before hurrying up the ridge.

They'd been working hard, their bodies weary, but they'd make it...if the fire held off long enough.

Matt glanced at his watch. One-thirty in the afternoon. The hike down had taken him almost an hour. By three, the air would be superheated and a flash fire could occur. Matt wanted to be far away from this canyon by that time.

"Have we got everyone on your crew?" he asked Jim Baylor, the crew boss, once he reached the end of the fire line.

"Yes, that's everyone."

"Then let's go."

Matt and Jim brought up the rear. It took the crew over an hour of hard climbing to reach the chopper. He and Jim helped load the men and women three at a time into the small plane. It took approximately eighteen minutes for the plane to fly down the mountain, drop off the fatigued crew members and fly back up for another load. They had twenty people to get down off this death trap.

"We can't go downhill because that'll take us into the fire, and we can't go up because we can't move fast enough to escape the blaze. It'll overtake us first," Matt said. "While the chopper flies crew members down the mountain, let's clear a burnout area where we can take refuge."

"Sounds like a good plan," Jim agreed.

While the chopper flew off the mountain with the first load of men, the rest of the team hustled, everyone working as hard as their tired bodies could move. One of the most important rules of wildfire fighting was to have an escape route at all times.

"The terrain is so difficult to work in that our crew has only been able to complete just under four chains of fire line an hour when we should have completed six chains," Jim said.

That was about two hundred and sixty-four feet an hour. Not much headway. Considering the rough terrain, Matt wasn't surprised.

He did the math, figuring how long it would take to get them all out of here. They didn't have much time. Matt was experienced enough to know what would happen if they were still here by late afternoon.

Two hours later, all of the crew had been moved off the mountain except for Matt and Jim. The chopper hovered just above the ground, never quite landing. Matt would be the last off the mountain. Nine minutes more and he could be with Andie again. He'd be safe.

And that's when he heard the loud rushing sound, like a freight train headed straight toward him. He'd heard it before, but he hadn't expected it to occur again this close and personal.

Matt turned and looked behind him, his body prickling with dread. A wall of flame exploded up the canyon. For one brief moment, he imagined glowing eyes and sharp teeth as the gaping maw reached toward him.

"Go! Run!" Matt yelled at Jim.

The man dived toward the open doors as a blast of hot air pushed against them. The chopper lifted off. His body pumping with adrenaline, Matt ran and jumped, wrapping his arms around the landing skid of the helicopter. Once again, he gave thanks for his Nomex gloves.

His body jerked and his booted feet dragged in the dirt, but he hung on. Then he felt himself flying through the air, but he didn't let go. He gripped the metal bar in a death grip, lifting his legs to cross them around the skid. He hung there. Nothing could wrench him away but death.

His helmet fell from his head, plunging into the flames below. He felt the heat of the fire licking beneath him, reaching for him. Trying to pull him in.

Breathing hurt, like swallowing fire. He ducked his head to protect his face and lungs, an instinctive gesture of survival. Tucking his face down, he used his teeth and shoulder to tug his red face shroud up over his mouth and nose.

Closing his eyes, he didn't look down. Didn't move at all. Just felt the rush of wind and heat against his body as he flew through the air, hanging on like a rag doll.

All he could think about was Andie and Davie. Seeing them again. His beloved family.

He was in God's hands now.

Chapter Seventeen

When the call came in from Matt that he'd found the hotshot crew, Andie breathed a sigh of relief. For several hours, she'd been jumpy, listening to every scratchy radio transmission, longing to hear Matt's voice again.

Finally. Finally he was preparing to come back. Evacuation had begun. Soon he'd be safe.

She watched the movements of the fire beneath Echo Canyon as the rolling flames swelled around the lower valley. The irregular winds buffeted the firefighters, fanning the flames higher and hotter. The fire crews had kept the fire from spreading through the valley to the local ranches, but they couldn't stop it from broiling up the canyon.

Matt was up there. She wanted him out, right now.

Please, God. Bring my husband home safe.

She repeated the prayer over and over again, holding it close to her heart. When the small chopper delivered the first three fire-crew members safely back at the command center, Andie cheered with everyone else. Word had spread fast amongst the fire crews and other personnel that they had some of their own in danger, and everyone was on high alert. As the chopper landed, they all grinned and clapped each other on the back, their hearts filled with the knowledge that it could be them in danger. It created a bond between them all, even though they might not know one another personally.

Andie didn't leave the helipad, determined to greet her husband the moment he landed.

Each trip by the chopper seemed to take a century. As each member of the evacuated fire crew landed and left the plane, Andie smiled and welcomed them home. She was happy they were safe, but they weren't Matt. They weren't the love of her life.

"The pilot says Matt is your husband. We're sure glad he came after us," one crew member said.

"Yeah, we wouldn't have known about the danger if he hadn't been there," another said.

Their gratitude touched her heart. What Matt had done wasn't an easy task. Adrenaline junky or not, he was an amazing man. A national resource because of his specialized training and skill level. A wildfire fighter.

She just wanted him back safe.

Radio malfunction and poor location was determined to be the cause of the communication breakdown. The hotshot crew had been low on batteries and hadn't checked their equipment well before departing.

Andie pressed the binoculars to her face, reluctant to be distracted for even a moment. Sweat trickled down her back, but she ignored it. As she watched the advance of the fire, a horrible foreboding washed over her. Matt would come out last. She knew her husband. He wouldn't leave until every other person was safely off that mountain.

"Oh, Matt. Come home, please. Come home to me," she muttered beneath her breath.

Finally the chopper only had two more men to bring down the mountain, and Matt was one of them. Ten more minutes and he'd be airborne, away from danger.

Safe.

And then the worst happened. So suddenly that Andie could only stare in astonishment. The fire exploded up the canyon, so loud she thought a freight train had sped up the mountain and crashed into a ball of flames. She jerked as the blaze shot skyward and billows of black smoke filled the sky.

No! Matt! He was still up there. Still in harm's way.

She sank to her knees, her legs too wobbly to hold her any longer. She knelt there in the dirt, her eyes wide with tears, her body visibly shaking. The entire camp went deathly quiet. Everything stopped. No one moved or spoke, their faces ashen with shock. They all looked east, toward the explosion. Knowing they had comrades still up there. Knowing they might be in mourning by evening.

Where was the chopper? Where was the last load of crew members?

Where was Matt?

And then Andie caught the low sound of a motor rising up above the roar of flames. A subtle sound, so weak she thought she must have imagined it.

The chopper appeared over the ridge, something dangling from one of its landing skids.

Andie pulled the binoculars up to her eyes, amazed by what she saw. A man clung to one of the skids with his arms and legs, hanging in midair as the chopper flew past the wall of smoke and bobbed down toward the staging area below. One stiff wind could easily dislodge the man and plunge him into the fire below.

"What on earth—?"

Who was it? How? Why?

People pointed at the sight, the subtle sounds of their comments filling the air along with the acrid stench of smoke.

And then Andie saw a flash of red below the man's head. A neck shroud. Used to protect the face and lungs from the choking smoke.

"Matt!" she screamed and came to her feet.

It was her husband. Clinging to the chopper like a lifeline. His body swept above the fire. If he let go, he'd plummet to his death.

Into the fire.

Voices permeated Andie's consciousness. People around her were waving and talking about the amazing sight. One man lifted his camera and started snapping pictures.

"This'll make the five-o'clock news," he crowed.

Matt. Somehow he'd gotten out of the fire. Somehow the Lord had brought him home. But he wasn't out of danger yet. If he let go…if a burst of hot wind struck him…if the chopper rocked unsteadily…

She couldn't think about that now. She had to be positive. Had to pray. He was going to make it. He was coming home to her.

The seconds ticked by like hours. Gradually, the chopper and Matt appeared larger. A crowd of firefighters surrounded the helipad, clapping and cheering as the chopper lowered enough so that Matt could drop off. But he didn't let go. With his body frozen in a death grip, he couldn't release his hold.

Several men ran to him, ignoring the whirring wind caused by the chopper blades overhead. Dirt sprayed Andie in the face and she felt the grit between her teeth, but she didn't shy away. She ran toward her husband, her cheeks awash with tears.

It took Matt several minutes to release his arms and legs. A few minutes for someone to help pry him off the skid.

Men carried him away so the chopper could land. Andie found herself beside Matt, clutching his hand, not knowing how she'd gotten there. Her legs must have moved of their own volition. She didn't know what to think. She only knew how she felt. Grateful. Relieved. Joyous. Overwhelmed. And so in love she couldn't even describe the emotion.

They sat Matt in a chair, a medic checking his vitals. He hung limp, his head rolling back as though the exertion of holding on had drained his body.

"Matt, oh, Matt!" she cried, hugging him tight.

"I'm okay. I'm fine." His voice sounded hoarse, like he'd breathed in too much smoke.

He looked dazed, his face black with soot. But she recognized the flash of his dear smile. The generous love in his clear blue eyes.

"Do you know where you are?" the medic asked.

"Of course. I'm safely out of the fire." He looked at Andie and grinned. "I came home to you, sweetheart. I kept my promise."

She laughed through her tears and kissed his filthy face. So happy to see him she was beside herself with relief.

"Don't you ever leave Davie and me again, Matthew Cutter. If you do, I'll hunt you down and drag you back," she warned.

He reached into his shirt pocket, his hand visibly shaking. He pulled out a rumpled yellow flower. It sagged on its bruised stem as he presented it to her. "For you, honey. I wanted you to know that even when I'm fighting wildfire, I'm still thinking of you. Only you."

He laid the limp flower on the palm of her hand, then closed her fingers around the stem and pressed a kiss to her knuckles. "I love you, Andie. More than life itself. And I'm not going anywhere."

As she kissed his lips, she knew what he said was true. They'd be together always.

She gazed into his eyes, her heart bursting with joy. "Come home with me, Matt. I want us to be a real family again. I love you so very much. I always have. Come home and be with Davie and me forever."

He smiled wide, his bloodshot eyes sparkling with happiness. He gave a harsh laugh, his voice sounding like a croak. "Finally. I thought you'd never ask."

"Neither did I. But Davie will be so happy."

"And what about you?" he asked.

She released a deep, satisfied sigh. "Yes—deliriously happy."

As she wrapped her arms around Matt and helped him stand, she realized what she said was true. She never thought it possible, but God had worked a miracle in her life. He'd restored her family. That which had been lost was now found. The love. The caring. The healing power of forgiveness. She had everything she could ever want or need.

* * * * *

Dear Reader,

Have you ever had a family member or someone very close to you who hurt your feelings desperately? I'm not talking about just a simple inconsideration, although those can certainly add up to bigger problems. But I'm talking about a serious infraction that can devastate a relationship.

They say blood is thicker than water. Families depend upon one another for support and solace. We have a natural love for our family members. We share special lifelong relationships with our family, but only the Savior is perfect. Surely during the span of our lifetime, we are bound to say or do something to hurt our family members. Likewise, they are bound to hurt us in return. For this reason, forgiveness is vitally important throughout our lives. If we don't forgive our family members, who will?

Sometimes we come from what is called a dysfunctional family. But I have discovered that no one has a "normal" family. Each family is so different. I have to be careful finding fault with other members of my family before I've looked at myself. We each should ask ourselves some questions before we judge others. What have I done or not done to exacerbate the problem? What have I said to hurt someone else's feelings? Have I accused them of forgetting to do something when

I likewise have forgotten to do things? Have I made them feel welcome and expressed my love and appreciation to them? Or have I only looked at their failings and imperfections? What about my own faults? Do I deserve to be shunned by them? Or have I looked the other way and forgiven them when they have hurt me?

In *The Forest Ranger's Husband,* both the heroine and the hero learn this lesson of forgiveness the hard way. According to the Gospel of John, none of us are without sin and we have no right to cast stones of blame at others until we have become humble enough to rid ourselves of our own faults. This doesn't mean we should become a doormat for a family member who might be involved in illegal activities or abusing us in some way. But it does mean we must become humble like unto a little child. Children are so forgiving. They want to see the good in everyone. Their pure innocence and kindheartedness serves as an example to all of us.

I hope you enjoyed reading *The Forest Ranger's Husband,* and I invite you to visit my website, www.LeighBale.com, to learn more about my books.

May you find peace in the Lord's words!
Leigh Bale

Questions for Discussion

1. In *The Forest Ranger's Husband,* Matt Cutter is a former hotshot, an elite wildfire fighter, and Andie is his estranged wife. After having a horrible argument, Matt leaves Andie to advance his own career goals. Do you think he was justified in leaving? Do you know people in your own family who have put their career ahead of their family? How can we keep from being so caught up in prestige and worldly goals that we ignore our family?

2. Andie acknowledges her fault in telling Matt to go away and she is finally able to forgive Matt for leaving her, but she has trouble trusting him enough to let him back into their marriage. Does forgiving someone mean we must also go back to the way things were?

3. There are many situations in a marriage that might require repentance and forgiveness, such as infidelity, physical or mental abuse, addiction, crime, etc. Sometimes these situations put the physical and mental well-being of our families at risk. Are there times when we should forgive a family member or friend, but not let them back into our life or return to the way things were? Why or why not?

4. Should we be more forgiving of family members than we are of friends and other people outside of our family? Why or why not?

5. When Matt goes to church for the first time, Andie ignores him, wishing he would stay away. Do you think her attitude was very Christianlike? Or do you think she was justified in her behavior when you consider her past history with Matt?

6. Have you ever been confronted at church by someone you disliked or had a bad experience with? How about out in the real world? How did you behave toward them? Should our behavior be different out in the real world versus how we act in church? Or should we behave the same no matter where we are?

7. After Aunt Susan hurts Davie's feelings by bad-mouthing his daddy, the little boy runs away. When Davie's mother finds him again, his uncle Brett tells them to do what families ought to do and forgive each other. Has anyone in your family ever hurt your feelings? Have you hurt them? Were you able to apologize and forgive each other and move on? How can you prevent grudge-holding within your own family?

8. Families have lifelong relationships together and are bound to get their feelings hurt at some point. How can you keep an open communication and forgiving heart within your family relationships? Are there limits to what we should forgive within our own family? Does forgiving a family member mean we accept their bad behavior?

9. While trying to win Andie's forgiveness for leaving her years earlier, Matt comes to realize that his love for her is not dependent upon her loving him. She has her free will to choose whether she loves Matt and how she will act. This revelation brings Matt peace because he chooses to love his family irrespective of how they feel about him. Have you ever chosen to be happy and love someone even though they were unhappy and did not return your love? How did your faith give you the courage to accept another family member's free will to choose for themself?

10. Have you ever forgiven a family member who hurt you either physically or mentally? Were you able to let them back into your life? Do you believe it was healthy to let them back into your life? Why or why not? Have you ever hurt a family member who later forgave you? Did

they welcome you back into their life? Why or why not?

11. How can we determine whether or not it is healthy for us to forgive someone and then welcome them back or omit them from our life?

12. In the story, Matt figures that most wives would bad-mouth their estranged or divorced husband, yet he is surprised to find that Andie has not done much of this. He is especially surprised to discover that Andie did not bad-mouth him to their son. Do you think it is appropriate for a wife or husband to say bad things to their children about their estranged or former spouse? Why or why not?

13. Andie comes to realize that Matt is suffering deep guilt and angst because he survived the wildfire when his crewman died. She doesn't want to help Matt deal with his grief, but neither can she turn her back on him when he needs her so much. Have you ever been compelled to help someone else who has hurt you deeply? What did you do?

14. Andie's sister, Susan, erases Matt's voicemail when he tries to contact his wife. Susan means well and is motivated by love and desire to protect Andie, but do you think what she did was

right or wrong? Have you ever interfered in family relationships to the point of making the situation worse? Has someone in your family interfered in your life before? How can we offer support to our close family and friends while not interfering or making the situation worse?

15. Matt is racked by survivor's guilt and also blames himself for his ruined marriage. By trusting in the Lord and putting his life in God's control, he realizes that he can choose to be happy, regardless of the bad things that have happened to him. Do you believe people can decide to be happy no matter what the circumstances? Or is it possible to be happy even when our lives fall apart? Why or why not?

16. Andie reaches the point where she just does not want to be angry at Matt anymore. When we withhold our forgiveness from someone else, does it hurt us, too? Is there a point when it hurts only us? Why or why not?

LARGER-PRINT BOOKS!

GET 2 FREE LARGER-PRINT NOVELS PLUS 2 FREE MYSTERY GIFTS

Love Inspired®

Larger-print novels are now available...

YES! Please send me 2 FREE LARGER-PRINT Love Inspired® novels and my 2 FREE mystery gifts (gifts are worth about $10). After receiving them, if I don't wish to receive any more books, I can return the shipping statement marked "cancel." If I don't cancel, I will receive 6 brand-new novels every month and be billed just $4.99 per book in the U.S. or $5.49 per book in Canada. That's a saving of at least 23% off the cover price. It's quite a bargain! Shipping and handling is just 50¢ per book in the U.S. and 75¢ per book in Canada.* I understand that accepting the 2 free books and gifts places me under no obligation to buy anything. I can always return a shipment and cancel at any time. Even if I never buy another book, the two free books and gifts are mine to keep forever.

122/322 IDN FEG3

Name _____ (PLEASE PRINT) _____

Address _____ Apt. # _____

City _____ State/Prov. _____ Zip/Postal Code _____

Signature (if under 18, a parent or guardian must sign)

Mail to the **Reader Service:**
IN U.S.A.: P.O. Box 1867, Buffalo, NY 14240-1867
IN CANADA: P.O. Box 609, Fort Erie, Ontario L2A 5X3

Not valid to current subscribers to Love Inspired Larger-Print books.

Are you a current subscriber to Love Inspired Larger-Print books and want to receive the larger-print edition?
Call 1-800-873-8635 or visit www.ReaderService.com.

* Terms and prices subject to change without notice. Prices do not include applicable taxes. Sales tax applicable in N.Y. Canadian residents will be charged applicable taxes. Offer not valid in Quebec. This offer is limited to one order per household. All orders subject to credit approval. Credit or debit balances in a customer's account(s) may be offset by any other outstanding balance owed by or to the customer. Please allow 4 to 6 weeks for delivery. Offer available while quantities last.

Your Privacy—The Reader Service is committed to protecting your privacy. Our Privacy Policy is available online at www.ReaderService.com or upon request from the Reader Service.

We make a portion of our mailing list available to reputable third parties that offer products we believe may interest you. If you prefer that we not exchange your name with third parties, or if you wish to clarify or modify your communication preferences, please visit us at www.ReaderService.com/consumerschoice or write to us at Reader Service Preference Service, P.O. Box 9062, Buffalo, NY 14269. Include your complete name and address.

LILP11B

Love Inspired®
SUSPENSE
RIVETING INSPIRATIONAL ROMANCE

Watch for our series of edge-
of-your-seat suspense novels.
These contemporary tales
of intrigue and romance
feature Christian characters
facing challenges to their faith...
and their lives!

**AVAILABLE IN REGULAR
& LARGER-PRINT FORMATS**

For exciting stories that reflect traditional values,
visit:
www.ReaderService.com